Laughton Osborn

The School for Critics

A comedy, being in completion of the fourth volume of the dramatic

series

Laughton Osborn

The School for Critics
A comedy, being in completion of the fourth volume of the dramatic series

ISBN/EAN: 9783337051631

Printed in Europe, USA, Canada, Australia, Japan

Cover: Foto ©Andreas Hilbeck / pixelio.de

More available books at **www.hansebooks.com**

THE SCHOOL FOR CRITICS

A COMEDY

BEING IN COMPLETION OF THE

FOURTH VOLUME OF THE DRAMATIC SERIES

BY

LAUGHTON OSBORN

> Sed hic stilus haud petet ultro
> Quemquam animantem; . . . . . .
> *   *   *   *
> . . . . at ille
> Qui me commôrit (*Melius non tangere!* clamo)
> Flebit, et insignis tota cantabitur urbe.
> HOR. *Serm.* II. 1.
>
> But not of my will seeks this steel point
> anyone living; . . . . . .
> *   *   *   *
> . . . . yet that one
> My wrath who shall waken (*Better to touch not!* I clamor)
> Shall wail, through my song in the whole of the city made famous.

NEW YORK

JAMES MILLER, 647 BROADWAY

MDCCCLXVIII

THE NEW YORK PRINTING COMPANY,
81, 83, *and* 85 *Centre St.*,
NEW YORK.

THE SCHOOL FOR CRITICS.

―――――

It is not my fault that this comedy is written. I should willingly have been at peace even with the small pretenders who prototype its characters; but they would not let me. All the personal conse-quences of its publication must rest with me alone. My book-seller has in it no interest but that of a commission-merchant, — which is less than some of its famous persons enjoy in the abortion and assignation advertisements of their daily issue.

L. O.

321 West Nineteenth-Street.

January 26, 1868.

THE SCHOOL FOR CRITICS

OR

A NATURAL TRANSFORMATION

MDCCCLXVII — VIII

CHARACTERS

SUS MINERVAM, *A.M., LL.D.; Editor of the* Ethnical Quarterly Review.

ANICULA, *Editress, under Bodkin, of the* Ethnos.

FLEDGLING, *Literary Critic, under Flunky Weathercock, of the* Hotchpot Hours.

DEADHEAD, *Literary Critic, under Polyphemus, of the* Hotchpot Cryer.

HEARTANDHEAD, *a retired Author and Critic.*

ATTICUS, *Literary Reader for the* Brookbank Publishing-house.

GALANTUOM, *Literary Critic of the* Hotchpot Civis.

SALTPETER,
BRIMSTONE, } *Underground gentlemen, on a mundane excursion.*
CHARCOAL,

SCENE. *Slanghouse-Square and its neighborhood, in Hotchpot City.*

TIME. *That occupied by the action.*

THE SCHOOL FOR CRITICS

Act the First

SCENE. *A street, at its opening into Slanghouse-Square.*

Enter

BRIMSTONE, SALTPETER *and* CHARCOAL, *encountering.*

Brim. Well, old Salt (since our Hell-coin'd names,
  Nor our Heaven-stamp'd either, can here be given),
  Missest thou not those jolly blue flames,
  Which, though — not quite as soft
  As the smokeless rays aloft
  In the region men call Heaven —
  They kept us mostly waking
  With a something like heart-aching,
  And never promis'd slaking
  Like the one day Earth's hell claims

For a solace out of seven,
Yet were bliss supreme, I swear,
To the weariness we are driven
To encounter in this air?

Salt. The weariness! disgust.
Why, Brim, thou 'rt losing fire.
Man's treachery, his lust,
His ferocity —— What boots
Comparing them with brutes?
These things wake mirth, not ire.
The trait which stirs my spleen
Is to find the beast so mean.

Brim. But then own it, as is just,
All Hell holds no such liar.

Char. That is because we have no Press.
Although we dabble so largely in steam,
We cannot throw off ream by ream
Of lies and nonsense, I must confess.
'T is an institution that should be ours.
Its sire was help'd by the Devil they say.
I saw on the wall of a house one day
A picture announcing a new old play.
A printing-press stood in the sky,
Held up by a cloud, while on a floor,
In a redtail'd coat which he never yet wore,
Stood who do you think old Faust before,
And pointed to the machine on high;
Who but the chief of the Infernal Powers?

Salt. Had the thing been stuck in a hole below,

It had show'd too plainly its use you know,—
As they use it here in Slanghouse-Square.[1]
Char. What name is that?

     Salt. One of apery, .
In all humility stolen, I hear,
By the loose-hing'd Weathercock quivering here,
From his ponderous model across the sea.
In front is the palace in rogues abounding,
Who draw from the public pot their fare,
And openly and at all times dare
What to us is perfectly astounding,
Who scent more filth in this upper air
Than would cover all Hell and leave to spare
Out of its fathomless superabounding.[2]

  On that right-hand corner, half sharp, half flat,
With perpetual simper and old white hat,
The rider of hobbies plies his trade,
Who thinks the rest of mankind were made,
At least that are male,
To be led by the nose and follow his tail.
Ambitious and hankering for display,
But not so genteel
By a very great deal
As Flunky Weathercock over the way,
He joy'd to become an arch-traitor's bail,
And journey'd far
To the Southern star
To take the seraphical man by the hand
Who fill'd with ashes and blood this land.

Char. I understand.

'T was an offer for station.

Brim. A bid for the votes of the Southern nation,
  When they come again to have command.
  He wanted to cut the Union in two,
  And would do it in four,
  If so it would give him three chances more
  To set his white head white and black heads o'er, —
  Which is what the Weathercock would not do.

Salt. They are going to make an envoy, they say,
  Of Flunky.

          Brim. Aha!   That is why, one day,
  To get appointed,
  To the People's Anointed
  He veer'd, then the next, to be confirm'd,
  To the People's deputies daintily squirm'd,
  And turn'd his tail the other way ?[3]

Salt. But let him alone, he is not our game.
  He is mean enough, like his fellows around,
  To put, if unseen, his nose in the ground,
  But sets too much store by an honest name
  (That bauble, you wot, human knaves have found
  To dazzle fools and their wits confound)
  To eat dry sawdust and swallow flame.
  Behind you, — turn round, —
  There is Bodkin's *Ethnos,* that olio sheet
  Where stale pretension and jargon meet,
  Affected science, dogmatic cant, .
  And ignorance glaz'd by amusing rant,

And what to us three makes its charm complete,
An air of candor, high-pitch'd yet sweet,
Which Sus Minervam himself can't beat.
'T is there we are bound.

Char. For what?

    Salt. Thou shalt see.

If the little old woman, whose girls there prepare
The dirty linen for public wear,
Should prove short-handed and pitch on me,
Why then Sus Minervam, A.M., LL.D.,
May add three points to his double degree.
Come, Charcoal, Brim, let us onward fare.

Brim. But give us to know of this mystery.

Char. And what our Master may want of us three.

Salt. So 't is something to do,
  What recks it? You two
Are weary like me of this sluggish air.
But this much is given
Ye both to know:
There is a fellow who wrote of Heaven
And human wo
And all that stuff of the Cross you know,
Who has ventur'd a dip in the lake below
And fish'd us up, to give us brains.

Brim. What an impudent gift!

    Salt. More than ye think.

To make us ramble like men in drink,
With fustian phrases and sense obscure,
Would picture us falsely, to be sure,

But would be worth the pains:
For fustian maintains our name's illusion
With man who is dazzled by word-confusion,
And finds magnificent and grand
All that his noddle can't understand,
And weighty the thoughts from whose tangled skeins
He fails to draw a conclusion.
Sus and Anicula, Fledgling too,
Though, like his master, he points both ways,
Help us a great deal nowadays
By keeping this great point in view, —
Save when his hireling pencil strays
From the false and absurd to what is true.

Char. So lucid Longfellow got his due.

Brim. Not when he labor'd to give to view
    The fanciful picture the Tuscan drew
    Of a place that is known to me and you.

Salt. Ay, Fledgling was then in his element,
    Serving the Devil with double intent:
    To lick up with neatness
    The spittle of greatness,
    And parade his own mock sentiment.
    Thus the uncouth phrase and the limping line
    Were held out to asses as grain divine,
    And stirring up rubbish he cry'd, "Oh fine!" *

Brim. What would ye have? Was not Swinburne's stuff,
    And Ruskin's and Emerson's affectation,
    And Carlyle's Dutch made bright enough
    To Fledgling's ratiocination?

Though the general mass of the reading nation,
Beating the thicket for explanation,
Might sooner guess at futurity,
Seeing we, who are us'd to what is tough
And the brightness that makes obscurity
In our underground relation,
Were wrapt in amaze
By the multiple blaze,
And lost our calculation.

Salt. Why you 've grown quite letter'd, old fellow Brim,
Since in coat and breeches here sojourning!

Brim. 'T is part of my universal knowledge.
I have the insight
By infernal right,
As Sus. got his at College.
I am not indeed A.M. like him,
Nor mean to purchase the other degree,
But I have an equal facility
In affecting all kinds of learning.
I think, had I a pen in hand,
And a cylinder press at my command,
Like Flunky, Brooks and Greeley,
I might do a devilish deal of good,
Like them, or the *World*, or Benjamin Wood,
Though I cannot lie so freely.

Salt. You shall do something better, and teach these fools,
Especially Sus, and Bodkin's piddler,
A lesson yet new in the Critics' schools,
That they who dance must pay the fiddler.

Char. Old fellow, well said:
>One would think you were bred
>An apprentice here in Slanghouse-Square.

Salt. 'T is the cruelest thing you could have said.
>I thought we devils had still some head,
>Despite of our brimstone air.
>But enough. Let us move. Ere the sun be gone
>To the West with his clouded nightcap on,
>Ye shall both of you see,
>And luminously,
>Into the pool of this mystery
>Whose bottom is visible only to me,
>And shall help me a comedy prepare.

Char. Amen! as said on his knees Jeff Davis,
>When he pray'd "From our enemies, O Lord, save us,
>And let them be damn'd!"⁶ So mote it be!
>I scent in the night-air a jolly spree.

Brim. Pitch and naphtha! (I hate to swear —
>But Milton taught me.) 'T will set us free
>From the chain of this damnable earth-ennui.

Char. And for the rest may the Devil care. [*Exeunt Diab.*

Enter
DEADHEAD *and* FLEDGLING.

Fledg. Well met, *Caput Mort.:* though our masters agree,
>Like two pickpockets, to scold each other,
>That is meant to blind the world, but binds not you and me.
>To us the phrase applies,

Crows pluck not out crows' eyes;
And we servants of the lamp,
Though we call each other scamp,
Yet, like beggars on a tramp,
Are each to the other hail-fellow and a brother.

Dead. Ay, 't is nuts to see the crowd,
Because we scold aloud,
Think both of us too proud
To shake each other's paw and swig hobnob together;
But, let it rain, old fellow,
They 'll find the same umbrella
Protects your stovepipe hat and my old felt from the
weather.

Fledg. Why, bravo! you improve:
That 's a figure now I love.
Don't be angry if I put it in my *Minor Notes* to-morrow.
Though, believe, I scorn to steal,
Save when hard-up for a meal,
Yet no one can object that now and then I borrow.

Dead. Very well; I 'll take my turn.

Fledg. Agreed. But I say, Dead, —
Ah, you know not how I yearn
To ask you on this head! —
Has your scribeship haply redd
The drama on the Cross
And those others ——

    Dead. — To our loss
Which some upstart bard ——

     Fledg. You err;

'T is an old hand at the game;
That is plain.   Besides, his name
Fits the collar of the cur
That snarl'd at us before
For the blackguard stuff we wore
And the lies we daily swore
In the Press.
As playwrights both ourselves,
Who have had our trash by twelves
Laid on the playhouse shelves,
'T is to Number One we owe it,
That our scorner, this d——d poet,
Lack success.
Have you redd him?

               Dead. 'Faith, not I.
Does it need to read, to damn?
Besides, old 'coon, I am,
Like yourself, prodigious shy
Of all writings where the style
Is above the common run,
Or where wit excludes low fun,
Nor the author has begun
To make it worth my while.
Fledg. I like your humor, but not your facts;
   You hint too plainly at certain acts
   Which we never commit in the *Hotchpot Hours*
Dead. The devil you don't!   Now, by the Powers,
   That is too cool.
   Do you take me, Fledgy, to be a fool?

Know not all men, do not all men see,

We differ in form, not in kind nor degree ?

For scandalous tales of vice and fraud,

And quack advertisements that serve the bawd,

And abortionists' invitations,

For all that debauches both soul and mind,

You are not an inch from us behind

And our counters might change stations.

Nay your Sunday sheet, which you loudly swore

Was the people to serve and would end with the war,

Peddles tales, as it spouted bombs before,

And is one of our institutions.

I should like to know what this all is for,

If it is not done to get you more

Of four-penny contributions ?

You know we are both rogues in fine ——

Fledg. In the world's sense, Heady, but not in mine,

Who hold that safety and honor bid, —

Here both combine, —

That we should of this high-topt fellow get rid,

Whose old-time light, that will not be hid,

Will clap on our bushel an extra lid,

And make it more hard to dine.

So be cautious, my jewel.

        Dead. Be not afraid.

For all some folk in the woods may deem **us**,

We never do nothing unless we are paid,

Me and my governor, Polyphemus.

Fledg. You 're right, by Jove. Had the cash been tipt,

I don't think any such flam had slipt

As those into which Bodkin's quarto dipt. —

Dead. No, none of us are so squeamous.[6]

Fledg. You are right, old boy, though your grammar is wrong.

But I 'm not much us'd to grammar myself.

The whole of Murray 's not worth a song.

It hampers genius; to get along,

All that we need is the love of pelf.

But let us be cautious, and keep to our tracks,

For our pride's defence ——

Dead. And the Revenue Tax.

You see I am sprightly and well may meddle

With playing my governor's second fiddle.

Are you off for your post? I am bound to mine,

Where opposite sandstone our marbles shine.

Fledg. Well, remember to give that fellow a line.

Dead. Be sure, if — you know — inspiration lacks.

Fledg. You need not read him: I sha'n't myself —

Save a page to seem knowing. Misrepresentation

Of authors, though blinding the innocent nation,

Lays never their critics on the shelf.

You know we stab behind their backs.

Our scraps will die, and ourselves unknown

Can indulge our malice and not be known :

None asks if a David have hurl'd the stone,

Or a ragamuffin beggar.

If the world but knew

It was I and you,

We should hardly dare say what we do,

And our pottage would prove *soupe maigre.*
It is such a delight,
To perch on a stool,
And write dunce and fool,
Under the shade of the veil'd gas-light,
And know on the morrow
The author in ire, or it may be in sorrow
If the creature is poor,
Has a sickly wife and a starving child,
Will find himself by a stroke of the pen ——
Dead. A stab in the back.
        Fledg. Ay, — for ever exil'd
From the coveted Eden of famous men,
And, door by door,
Seek in vain for a publisher evermore!
Is n't that to be mighty? It adds, my dear,
Breadth to our breast and a bead to our beer.
Dead. Let us have some, Fledgy.
        Fledg. You soul, I am here.

    Exeunt affectionately together.

A C T   T H E   S E C O N D

SCENE. *Anicula's Sanctum.*

Enter Sus MINERVAM.

Sus. Out? What a pity! It is more than a pity.
What shall I do? This monstrous Hotchpot City,
Too small a cradle for my pregnant fame,
Will frown indignant on my letter'd name,
If I, who am its snuff, its salt, its scalpingknife and cautery,
Lack pepper for this pupping quarter's Quarterly.
The case is bad, and there is no evasion.
She comes! I will address her grandly,
That she may listen to me blandly
And minister unto my great occasion.

Enter ANICULA.

Thou stay and glory of Bodkin's Press,
From its primal T to its ultimate letter,
O render me help in my sore distress,
And I'll be forever your debtor!
O et præsid'ium et dulcè decus' meum',
Have you no more "rejected", to give me some?
Shake up your old drawers, and find me a few

To swell out my Quarterly Review;
Oh do!

Anic. Plague on you, Sus! can't you scribble, yourself?
I sold you the last rubbish on my shelf.
There was the scandal of the Piedmont poet,
With its pretended knowledge and false taste,
And its translations, which, not done in haste,
Yet were so vapid that they seem'd to show it.
And there was the fustian stuff on Rowley,
Who is made to declaim so rantipolly,
While his critic agape cries "Grand! Sublime!"

Sus. Stop there, old angel. 'T was not my crime.
Little vers'd as I am in nature or art,
I saw both were outrag'd, from the start.
Amus'd at once, and not less astounded,
I fear'd all Hotchpot would be confounded,
At the time.
Have pity, that 's a dear good soully!
I am in such a muss,
And have shaken the dust from my wit-bag wholly.

Anic. Don't bother me, Sus.
My girls are at work, and 't is all they can do
To make shifts for me, let alone for you.
But I know of a means: it is *entre nous.*

Sus. Sure; I 'll take ten times my oath.

Anic. As you will not keep it, one time will do.
There is an odd fellow will serve us both.
He was here but now, will be here again. —

Sus. O my delight!
18*

Anic. Old boy, be quiet!
Would you rob my virtue?

     Sus. No, to be plain,
There is none of it left.

     Anic. You beast, I deny it.
I have lent it at times to you and to others,
Stock-gamesters and politicians bold,
But 't is as immaculate as my old mother's
The day I was foal'd. ~

Sus. Well?

   Anic. But hands off! This fellow, who is
A queer sort of devil and much of a quiz,
Works quickly and cheaply.   .

     Sus. Cheaply? O joy!
He may aid me for nothing!

  .   *Anic.* Very likely, my boy.
You are not very nice,
In phrases or sense, ˙
(Which lessens the price,)
And if you dispense
With fixing the theme ――

     Sus. Let him scrawl what he will,
So I have not to pay and the scribble will sell.

Anic. In fact, he charg'd nothing for mine. .'T was a favor.
So I let him select. There 's a tragical shaver
Whom he wanted to crush, for making Hell logical,
For giving man's passions to Judas Iscariot,
For not putting Christ in a fiery chariot,
And, with syntax and prosody,

Which ought not in the Cross to be,

Bowing respect to laws etymological.

Sus. Heh! heh! that is funny!

A similar jumble came posted to me.

And as the confector requested no money ——

Anic. Confectioner.

> *Sus.* No. 'T is confector I mean.

I us'd the phrase learnedly, wittily too,

With a double-entendre quite fresh, smart, and clean,

As, in one of its senses, your *Webster* will show. —

Anic. But you spoke of a jumble,

> *Sus.* And it was one, I trow,

A jumble, old woman, to you and to me.

As the mixer was flippant enough to seem airy,

I stitched him with Rowley and Victor Alfieri,

In my last Quarterly, — which see.

It is there as it reach'd me, and in no wise doth vary

Except in the learning which fits LL.D.

Anic. 'T was the same fingers doubtless that jumbled for me.

Mine was sheer lies from beginning to end.

Sus. And mine. Greater nonsense there could not well be.

Not even boy Chatterton's trumpery

Was worse. But still 't was the Devil's god-send,

That nondescript mishmash on *Calvary.*

Anic. Mum! Fledgling comes. Don't be tempted to brag

Of our gratis co-worker. Do as you see me.

Sus. I will do as befitteth my double degree,

Rest assur'd, ma'am, nor let the cat out of the **bag.**

Enter FLEDGLING.

Anic. Good day, Fledgling Minor.

                Fledg. Old dame, how do' do ?
    You have done a fine thing. Sus Minerv', how are you ?
    I thought to praise one, and I find two instead.
    But as your duality,
    In this critical matter
    Whereof I would chatter,
    Presents but a unity in its reality,
    You are both so alike
    In what both have said
    (Believe not I flatter ;
    Any fool it would strike
    As well as myself in my strong ideality),
    You have lost, sir and ma'am, each the nice speciality'
    Of individuality,
    And, a great generality,
    I may group the totality
    Of my *pensées* on both on this point 'neath one head.

Anic. Little Fledgy, you 're learning,
    I see, in your yearning,
    Your proud spirit burning
    And claws of earth spurning,
    Your small wings to spread.
    You 've consulted Ralph-Waldo, I opine, on that head.
    Excuse me for going. As Sus and I
    Are to be in your panegyric blended,
    What is aim'd at him, if for both intended,

Will hit me too in the very eye.

You have left I see your Minor key

And are strumming it largely on Major-C.

But pray don't take either of us for a flat,

While playing your sharps.　Sus, remember the cat.

[*Exit.*

Fledg. What does the harridan mean by that?

Sus. I vow'd not to tell.

But as in the *Hours* — 't was on Sunday, 't is true;

That is Flunky's venality, comes not of you —

But as in the *Hours* you quoted me freely,

Much more so than Greeley,

And so made me sell,

I will tell you in confidence;

But do, pray, be on your fence,

And not the fact spill.

Fledg. To one only, — Deadhead.

Sus. Him only then. —　Well,

What is the stuff which we write so alike upon?

Fledg. " Virginia " and " Calvary."

Sus. Homer, and Dante —— No, the Devil —— You see,

There 's an odd sort of fellow we both chanc'd to strike upon,

Who made the same nonsense for both him and me.

But I improv'd mine, as behoov'd my degree,

And made my points good

By Fernando Wood,

As evidence of my Latinity.

Fledg. Made your points good!　Unmade them, you mean.

Why even Fernando would beat you there clean,
Or, as Dante's great double would say, "*dead* beat."
What a phrase is that![8] — If you want to lie
Against an author, you should not quote,
My little old fellow, but do as did I
In my Minor Note, —
For his language I knew would reveal the cheat.

Sus. Don't call me old; for I 'm yet in my prime.
I am perhaps little, but oh! sublime.
What I said then of Homer and Virgil and Dante
Proves my knowledge and genius, albeit 't was scanty.

Fledg. It had better been out though, or laid on the shelf
For another occasion, for on my blind soul,
Though I don't know much of those Grecians myself,
As my time is not given to study but pelf,
There was nothing of fitness or sense in the whole.
The exordium of an epic tale
And the opening scene of a tragedy,
Although, like the multiple flimsy thread
The spider passes from out her tail,
They may both be spun from a single head,
Are not the same web any dunce may see,
Nor was there the least concinnity
In all the rest you said.

Sus. Why do you prate thus unto me?
Am I not an LL.D. ?
And A.M. too, as it is express'd ?
A fledgling — not of your family,
But of that lofty scholastic nest,

Which in all countries, as late I said,
And in all ages, — before there were
Or scholars or schools, you may infer,
Where fools are taught to scribble for bread, —[9]
On its annual brood is made to confer ——

Fledg. Gratis?

       Sus. O no! that were to err —
Those letters which at our tails attest
We are ting'd of the color of the dead.

Fledg. But that must be hard?

           Sus. Hard! Look at me.
See how I flourish my double degree.
There is nothing I give to the world, my dear,
But there my tailpieces both appear,
To signify my brains are Scar;
Yet I am not paler, as you may see,
Than if I belong'd not to the blest.
In Heidelberg, so runs the tale,
Where they keep these tickle-me-ups for sale,
A British noble got LL.D.
Conferr'd on his horse.[10]

       Fledg. You joke.

         Sus. 'T is true.

Fledg. Why not his ass?

       Sus. Had he so thought best.
And why not as well as for you or me?
A letter'd ass — "haud absurdum est."
'T is "*facere* well reipublicæ." [11]

Fledg. What 's all that gibberish?

Sus. Learned words

I wear at top, like Panza's curds,

To keep my brainpan soft and warm.

They have no meaning, but do no harm,

And help my LL.D. A.M.

Whenever I sport that double degree, —

Which is four times a year; and you must admit

There is not an ass it would better fit,

I bray so mellifluously.

But that is self-praise.   But, you made me warm.

Fledg. Excuse, old fellow : I meant no harm.

Here, shake our fist.

There is one thing, however, we all forget :

This bard, they say, is a satirist,

And may turn the tables on us yet.

Though I fear not, I ;

For Duyckinck, on whom we may rely, —

His book is a great one — bigger by half

Than Webster's, or the Bible ;

Some of the copies are bound in calf! ——

Sus.   A feature perhaps to make one laugh,

Who knows that its censure is mostly chaff

And its praises are a libel.

Fledg. It may be so.   I never read

Such gallimaufries, not I indeed ;

I should grope there in vain for fruit or seed

To stock my garden of *Minors.*

But Duyckinck says, he had no success,

His *Vision* " fell stillborn from the press ; "

 Perhaps because he lack'd cleverness,
 Not to shine, but to use the shiners.

Sus. Then Duyckinck says what is not true,
 And what *could* not be such he very well knew,
 As is patent to me, though not to you
 Who were yet in the nest. But the fact is this:
 The hairy babe was a bouncing boy,
 And crow'd and laugh'd to his daddy's joy,
 And to the heirless neighbors' annoy,
 Who envied him his bliss.
 But he found ere long its nurses were cheats:
 They took their wages, but spar'd their teats,
 To feed their own brood which did not pay.
 So the father took the child away.

Fledg. In plainer words?

      Sus. He stopp'd the sale,
 By cutting off the book's supply:
 A fact he himself took care to imply
 At a somewhat later day.
 Such books as that do not often fail.
 It is true, neither you nor I was then
 In the trade which puts down rising men,
 Although there was then black-mail.
 You may judge though Duyckinck's malignity,
 From the misspell'd name at the article's top
 To the close where he calls him a travel'd fop,
 And has the astounding audacity,
 For a work like that, and from such as he,
 To deny him, except as an oddity,

A niche in his hall of letters.
I know not what other men may think, —
Some find sweet odors in things that stink, —
But it would not be with his betters.

Fledg. Hi! hi! do you laud him thus? yet choose
To scribble him down?

                    Sus. Not more I deem
Than others in heart have done and do
Who find a pleasure like curs, it would seem,
In lifting the leg at a profitless muse,
While they yelp as a publisher's puffer;
Than *Ethnos*, the long *Round Robin*, and you,
And your ape across the Eastern stream,
The *Wart-City Buzzard's* stuffer.
However, the fellow should be content,
If he is only a curious ornament
To which Heaven has nothing substantial lent,
As with Milton, or even with Beattie,
That the Barnum of letters has spar'd him a nook
In the rummage-drawer showshop for general look,
His two-volume Cyclopedci'acal book
Of American literati.

Fledg. So, so; that is frank. And yet yet you admit
Against him what neither has sense nor wit!
Was it done in a Duyckinckish splenetic fit,
Or is it your love to scoff?

Sus. For an ass, you have got in the highway for once.
Like you, I love to call "Dull!" and "Dunce!"
It makes one seem sensible for the nonce.

Then, I hop'd he would buy me off.

Fledg. You try'd that game against the College.

But Præses your hints would not even acknowledge,

And sneer'd both Freshman and Soph. —

But why did you not, for deception's sake,

Between your nonsense a difference make

And the stuff in Bodkin's quarto?

The faults in grammar and English alone,

Without the falsehoods and impudent tone

And puerile pertness, would any one strike

As drawn from one ditch: in fact, they are like

As Port is to Oporto.

Sus. What matters it?   The world may say

What it likes; it may call you Beaumarchais;

Me Pindar, or Greeley Cupid:

'T is known I buy up all hackney'd and **tame**

Rejected articles.   Where is the blame?

They 're the only stuff for which I pay,

At least in the literary way,

And I 'ld swear the *Ethnos* does the same,

Though it never was else than stupid.

Fledg. In one thing, though, you may claim to be

More than its match.

　　　　　　　　Sus. In hypocrisy?

Why yes, in that, and post-mortem scandal,

No prick-fame can hold to me a candle.

The Round-Robin try'd it on *Calvary,*

Which he damn'd with a slaver of sympathy,

And smil'd like a king benignant:

But 't is Bowery-acting to my pretence
Of friendliness and benevolence,
Where impertinent and malignant.
You try'd it in the post-mortem line,
And fancy'd you'd done it egregiously fine,
When out of your press issu'd Byron a swine;
But look how I Circe'd Alfieri!

Fledg. 'T was done in my finest retributive mood,
Because Alger, in his *Solitude*,
Had blown him upward as extra good,
A kind of Castalian fairy.[12]

Sus. Eh! I thought you lik'd such soap-bubble stuff.

Fledg. When not too frothy, and *quantum suff.*

Sus. 'T is your Swinburne over again in prose,
But a little more liquid, with more repose,
And Emerson's verse without rhyming close
And a devilish deal less tough.[13]

Fledg. What then? we must worship such men, while yet
Their fame is up and their life not set:
In secret thinking, I go as you go,
And hold Ralph-Waldo, albeit my pet,
As pompous an ass as Victor Hugo,
Who seems to think it his right divine
To bray for all others asinine,
And, hating the right divine of kings,
Is in his pride and his ostentation,
His spirit of logical domination,
Elation and affectation,
The very tyrant he prates of and sings.[14]

Sus. Eu'ge! that 's truth without dilution.

    I cannot see how it got into your sconce.

    After that mouthful, my Minorite dunce,

    You may lie for a month and have absolution.

Fledg. But don't let out that it was my say :

    Such notions would ruin my trade at once.

    Here hobbles Anicula this way.

    I am off.   It is more than I can do,

    To parry and thrust both with her and with you.

Enter ANICULA.

    Good day, old lady ; I 'll in by and by,

    When no one can come 'twixt your beauties and I.

Anic. And me.

        Fledg. Never mind. You might pass the bad grammar,

    For the soft soap it carries. [*Aside.*] The impertinent!

        d—n her !

    'Bye, Sus Minervam, A.M., LL.D.

    The greatest critic that ever could be

    Would be one to unite

    The crepuscular glow of your learning's rushlight

    With Anicula's sterling vacuity.   [*Exit.*

Enter SALTPETER.

Anic. He has vanish'd in time, the magpie and ape. —

    Here enters a beast of another shape,

    And bird of another feather.

'T is the gentleman who,

I mentioned to you,

Would do for us both together.

Let me make you acquainted.

This short sturdy man, who looks like a fool,

Is not so, Mr. Salt, in despite of his jaws.

In the Heaven of letters he sings psalms to our sainted,

Gives pills in our critico-purgative school,

And is Master of Arts and a Doctor of Laws.

Salt. What 's his name ?

    Anic. Sus Minervam.

      Salt. A great one.

        Anic. A beater !

Sus. And pray what is yours ?

    Salt. Mine is simple Saltpeter.

Sus. That 's *The cart draws the horse.*

As we say it in Latin,

Bovem' trahit currus : but ox falls less pat in.

Peter Salt, not Salt Peter, I take it of course.

Salt. No, it is as I tell you.

    Sus. Then *Salt,* I opine,

Was the name of your mother.

    Salt. No mother was mine.

Sus. Then your father's.

    Salt. I had none.

      Sus. A foundling, ha, ha !

A bastard ?

   Salt. If 't please you. Like others, I know not

The source of my being, though not blind to my true lot.

For aught that I know, I might claim for papa

That doughty Apostle whose thin blade 't is said

Circumcis'd Malchus' ear

Without shaving his head.

Sus. You mean your papa's oldtime foresire, 't is clear.

As his name too was Simon,

That 's a poor stock to climb on,

And, without amphibology,

Your Scripture chronology

Has been, Mr. Salt, much neglected, I fear.

Salt. Be that as it may,

This truly I say:

Like yourselves, I came into this world without will;

But, unlike yourselves, when I find I 've my fill,

I shall haste to go out of it, of my accord,

So soon as my governor whispers the word.

Sus. Who is your governor? 'T is not the Lord?

You don't look so pious.

                                    Anic. No, to judge by his eye,

One would think some one else had his Saltship for ward.

Sus. I like him for that; that fire would imply

He 's a deuse of a fellow.

                                 Salt. I am. Will you try?

I work on long credit; sometimes gratis, you 'll find.

Does it suit, who my governor is never mind.

You will both of you know him at no distant day.

He keeps long accounts, and, as you 've seen by the sample,

Has taught me to follow his princely example,

·And be not exacting for present pay.

Sus. You 're a jewel of a man, Peter Salt or Salt Peter.
  Let us strike up a bargain.

Anic. My girls call me out.

  I 'll be back to you soon.   [*going.*

Sus. [*aside.*] Salty dear, don't entreat her

To stay with us.   Both will do better without.

[*Exit Anic.*

You must know —— Don't betray me !

Salt. No, word of a devil !

Sus. What an oath !   What an odd fish you are !

You must know,

  Our lady-friend's intellect 's under the level :
  She is not an A.M., as I was long ago, —
  (I 'm a Doctor of Laws too, my Quarterlies show.)
  Therefore put off on *her* all your flatness and drivel,
  If you have of those articles much to dispense.

Salt. Sus Minerv', LL.D., I would not be uncivil,
  But, except when I practice a little deception,
  They are products to which I can make no pretence.

Sus. They belong to the Dailies, I know, by prescription,
  And to Minor-Note Fledgling by eminence.

Salt. There was some, it is true, in the piece I last sent you,
  (I own it to show I would not circumvent you ;)
  But in future I 'll give you misrepresentation,
  Mock learning, bad syntax, and word-ostentation,
  A truly illogical argumentation,
  With a sparkle too of vituperation ;
  And o'er all and through all, and 'mid scintillation,
  Shall lie an amusing want of sense.

Sus. Dear Mr. Salt! As from sympathy

    You serv'd her for nothing, you will do this for me?

Salt. I will do it, dear Doctor, because it will be

    For my governor's delectation.

Sus. And for nothing?

                Salt. For nothing. But this is to say:

    Better count the cost before we commence.

    Though I charge not, the Devil may be to pay.

Sus. I am us'd to that in a general way:

    So make haste, and damn the expense.

Salt. But in all that I promise you flourish already.

    Mac'te virtu'te; be bold and be steady.

Sus. Ha, ha, you have learning! That is a new charm in you.

    I will make you my partner!

                Salt. I should prove rather warm for you.

    I use all the tongues of civilization

    By an anti-apos'tolic inspiration, —

    And certain more beside.

    But let us return to my observation,

    From which we are straying wide.

    You have in yourself all you ask me to give;

    But I 'll make you in letters the top of the nation,

    And your name for ever to live.

Sus. How, how, how?

Salt. Meet me about a half-hour from now.

Sus. Say where! O where?

Salt. In the Park, at the side on Slanghouse-Square.

    I will introduce you to two friends there

    Who will teach you to prick up your oars in the air.

      Vol. IV.—19

Sus. I 'm the happiest dog beyond compare!

Salt. Hush! here comes the old sow.

Be off now.

Sus. Bow, wow!

> *Sus gets upon all fours,*
> *makes a demi-wheel on his hands. and Exit*
> *yelping delightedly.*

ACT THE THIRD [16]

SCENE. *The Park fronting Slanghouse-Square.*

Enter

ATTICUS, HEARTANDHEAD *and* GALANTUOM.

Gal. Here lies my street, at the right. 'Let us stop.
Att. But not, for awhile yet, the question drop.
    Have you ever redd *Cato?*
                    Gal. To wonder and laugh.
    More than half is mere prose.
                    Att. And the rest of it chaff.
    There is nothing of nature in all, and the poet,
    If conscious of passion, was unable to show it.
    A schoolboy had written his love-scenes as well.
    To affect to compare then *Virginia* with *Cato,*
    Which has scarce one good part, save the passage on Plato,
    To name Rowe and Young, and the public to tell
    That our author was tutor'd in this or that school
    Is to read without books:
                    Gal. Or to talk like a fool.
    Why our tragedy-scribe, as the pert lady styles him
    Who does up the Ethnos' old linen for new,
    Has made his own school; though, while Round-Robins
        sell

And knaves that are Masters of Asses revile him,
He will have to wait long for a pupil or two.

Att. That is said very well.

In the teeth of the *prôneurs* of Swinburne and Ruskin,
He has dar'd to talk clearly, has taken from passion
Her stilts, and despite of prescription and fashion
Has refus'd to put monsters in sock or in buskin.
But not in his diction
And sentiments merely
Makes he Nature his guide ;
But in the connection
And sequence of incidents, where others clearly
Set nothing by space, be it little or wide,
And time with its intervals put quite aside.
And in costume not less,
In the manners and thought-modes which mark out each
    nation,   .
He has labor'd more faithfully such to express
Than any before him, without contestation,
Whate'er his success.
You, Galantuom, in your frank declaration,
Have sought to commend him as pure in his style.
I have honor'd him more.
He has swept clean the Stage which was filthy before,
And made men be merry without being vile.
Which is something still better, and I think more sublime,
Than his lifting his tones without word-ostentation
And compressing his Acts in the limits of time.

Heart. The *Round Robin* labor'd, knew not what to do.

Its conscience prick'd sore, but the author was new.

So it *damn'd with faint praise*, and, with impudent leer.

Affecting the gracious, *taught others to sneer.*

Gal. For the trait you mention,

That impudent air of condescension,

Which must have made our poet smile,

And reminded him of the plate where you see

Beside a mastiff a little cur sitting

On a footing of borrow'd equality,

With an air of consequence the while,

Which says as might words, if words were fitting,

"Don't mind that big fellow, but look at me.

I patronize him.   To a certain degree

You may let him have your attention." ——

Heart. I remember the print ; the inscription redd,

"Impudence and Dignity."

Had the artist the *Round Robin* in his head,

Feeling big, and trying to look full-bred,

With its little rump near *Calvary ?*

Gal. Well, so far as the trait you mention,

That funny assumption of condescension,

I am with you, but not in the good intention

You seem to assign that pretentious sheet.

Yet, in its preposterous conceit

It tells us serenely it holds him no poet!

Then quotes and misquotes, and, in order to show it,

Makes none of its righteous selections complete,

For fear that its readers should scent out the cheat!

Heart. You forget one act of liberal dealing.

It has honor'd the Devil, who is great in oration,
With a good long piece of declamation,
Which, it says, is the nearest to demonstration
The author makes of poetic feeling.

Gal. A piece of satirical reasoning! blent
With the kind of brimstone sentiment
At vogue in the underground dominion!
In rhyme too!

        Att. No doubt with a double intent, –
The style of the drama to misrepresent,
And offend the public opinion.
Had he been a true critic, he would have known,
However lofty may be its tone,
Impassion'd, pathetic, pointed or strong,
To dialogue Nature has rarely lent
What is call'd poetical ornament.
The noblest masters of tragic song
Have shunn'd it as shuns our author, and he,
By this truth of art and consistency,
May reap honor late, but will keep it long.

Gal. So I said, when extolling, what fools decry'd,
Those two first comedies of his.
His adherence to nature will not be deny'd
By those who know what nature is.
But Heartandhead differs.

        Heart. Not I indeed;
Those are main points in my critical creed.
But I think the Round Robin err'd not of will,
But spoke to the best of his knowledge and skill,

With the grandly unconscious droll conceit
In letters of all such empirics;
For we find him assign
The afflatus divine,
Which he could not feel breathe in a single line
Of our author's most polish'd drama,
Where think you ? (it is to take by its bleat
A bob-tail sheep for a lama)
To — oh the amazement! and oh the fun !
To travesty-singing Conington,
Who makes the lord of hexameter verse
His stately and deep-mouth'd epic rehearse
In *Marmion's* four-foot lyrics.
This shows that, though better in sense and breeding
Than Flunky Weathercock's scribbling-man,
Robin knows not what poetry is, and the plan
With its incongruity exceeding
Was nothing strange to the purblind possessor
Of respect for an Oxford Latin-professor.

Gal. All which is true.

But, beginning to quote what well he knew
Was both lofty in tone and ornate too,
Why did he stop ?   Because intent
To keep from the light his false argument. [16]

Heart. Yet he gave, spread out to the public view,
A foremost passage.

Gal. Ah ! did he so ?

Your own kind nature makes you slow
To detect, beside ignorance. malice.

    Quem-Deus-vult-perdere reckon'd o'er
    The fourteen true verses, then stupidly chose
    To invite their contrast with Knowles's four
    Of vulgar, half-rythmical, fustian prose ;
    No doubt to our poet's amus'd delight,
    For he took the pains both pieces to cite
    In a note to his story of *Alice.* [17]

Heart. I fear you are right.

Att. Yet you, Heartandhead, in a just cause have done
    More to baffle these fools than of us either one,
    Although you have done it in vain.
    Galantuom wrote honestly, therefore well,
    But he did but his duty in his vocation.
    And on me a like obligation fell
    In a different situation.
    I fulfill'd it too ; but in part with pain ;
    As could not but be,
    Since I hold the theme of *Calvary*
    Too awful for human brain.
    But you, Heartandhead, who had given up long
    The critic's function wherein you were strong,
    As declare both Poe and Irving,
    Without hope of renown took up agen
    Your kindly and truthful and graceful pen,
    To write back these false or misguided men
    To the path from which they were swerving.
    But the *Nightly Pillar* was deaf as a post. —

Heart. Or something worse, for it kept me tost
    On hopes and doubts, afraid to say nay,

Yet loath to assent, till, my patience lost,
And asham'd to be put off day by day,
I told him my mind, and in sheer disgust
Took the manuscript bugbear away.
It was worse however with Weathercock's olio;
For Flunky is master; the youth is not,
Who does small chars for the dames of Hotchpot
In the *Nightly Pillar's* folio.
Flunky stammer'd and shuffled, and talk'd of space;
Yet my piece was brief, but in eulogy,
Which did not with his views agree,
Although I gave him to understand
The poet had never seen my face.

Gal. I think it might have alter'd the case,
Had you gone with cash in hand.

Heart. Not with Flunky.

     Gal. I know not that: the men
Who daily damn souls, for simple gain,
By their lust-tales and calls to abortion,
Would scarce be affected by shame or with pain,
That a critical piece by a classical pen
Should pay in their sheets its proportion.

Att. Well? He stammer'd and shuffled — revolving, no doubt,
How, an old acquaintance, he might get out
Of the mesh of your application.
'T is the Weathercock's weakness, as is known,
To vibrate, by opposite winds when blown,
On his pivot of gyration.

Heart. And to turn over patiently stone after stone,
  19*

  To explain his tergiversation.

Gal. Why true; but he 's quite outdone in that
  By the greasy saint in the old white hat,
  Who is like Val Jean in the *Misérables,* —
  Who, liken'd to Christ in the strife for good,[12]
  Yet tries more tricks to get out of the wood
  Than any beast in Fontaine's *Fables.*

Att. Well, — he shuffled and stammer'd and talk'd of space ——

Heart. To consider how best he might with grace
  Refuse.

   Gal. Which must have made you smile
  For a half-breed of the mongrel journals,
  Us'd to the haste,
  The scissors and paste,
  Of his piebald minute-liv'd diurnals,
  To choke at an essay of yours.

     Heart. Meanwhile,
  The poet got wind of my design,
  Through a mutual friend, and thinking, 't may be,
  Qui facit per alium facit per se,
  Begg'd, that for his sake, as well as mine,
  I would withdraw it definitively.

Gal. 'T was a false pride, I think.

     Att. No, he who wrought
  Virginia, and thinks what his Ernestin taught,
  Could do no less, it appears to me.

Heart. But is it not strange, this hostility
  In the hounds of the Press?

     Gal. 'T is a personal **quarrel.**

Who wrote *Rubeta* and *Arthur Carryl*

Deserv'd no mercy, you must confess.

Head. Not had he libel'd by falsehood, as they.

Gal. " The greater the truth, the worse the libel."

To prove your foes false, yet in what you say

Be yourself the Bible,

Is to turn on their foulness the glare of day.

Att. But who of these asses first open'd the bray

Gal. The *Ethnos'* old lady, who spins a long yarn.

Then the Master of Asses himself, who, they say,

Buys all her old fodder to store in his barn.

The result is so like, not alone in the strain

Of shameless untruth, but assumption vain,

They have had the same devil at work, 't is plain,

Whoever may be to pay.

Heart. Let us go to the *Ethnos* and find how it is.

Att. I 'm not known ——

   Heart. But I am to the petticoat quiz.

'T is worth the essay.

Come, Gal'ant.

   Gal. Not now. As I told you, yon street,

Where the *Civis* is, calls me away.

But, in less than an hour, I will both of you meet

At Anicula's.

   Heart. Well then.

     Gal. Good day.

ACT THE FOURTII

SCENE. *As in Act III.*

SUS. SALTPETER. BRIMSTONE. CIIARCOAL.

Sult. These are my friends. Let me make you known.
    Gentlemen, this is the great A.M. ——
Sus. And LL.D.
        Salt. And LL.D.,
    Who by natural right of his double degree,
    And that alone ——
Sus. No, my Quarterly.
Salt. And his quarterly sheet of motley knowledge,
    To learning and letters makes more pretence
    With an infinitesimal dose of sense,
    Than was ever yet made, or will be hence,
    Out of a Freshman's class at college.
    Doctor Sus Minervam.
                Sus. Gentlemen both,
    I am not at all proud, being us'd to praise, —
    So am happy to make your acquaintance.   Though loath,
    Permit me first a question to raise.
    What are your names?   Mr. Salt forgot,
    Too full of me, and my titles God wot,
    To name the characters in his plot.

Salt. This gentleman then, with the fiery nose,
 Is Mr. Brimstone, dull quiet stuff,
 If he only would keep cool enough ;
 But he is very apt to get blue.
 The other in the iron-gray clothes,
 And with so swart a hue,
 Is a light and spongy fellow, like you,
 Yet with a fibre you can't see through,
 Though neither solid nor tough.
 His name is Charcoal.

     Sus. And yours Saltpeter !
 With such a three,
 It appears to me,
 Unless you 're a most outrageous cheater,
 It hardly is safe to keep company.

Salt. That might be in another place.
 But here, unless you carry fire,
 You 're as safe as you would be in the mire
 Of your own journal's dirtiest place.

Sus. That is safe enough ; for I scarcely can keep,
 When I bogtrot there, my brains from sleep,
 And I get stuck fast, with big words and grammar,
 As often as waddling Anicula (d — n her !)

Salt. And now to business. But first, a word.
 Have you faith, Dr. Sus,
 That the spirit-world ever comes to us, —
 I mean to the men of this earth, — as averr'd ?

Sus. By whom ?

    Salt. By hysterical girls who are able

To talk with ghosts through the planks of a table
And see through the mop of their chignons.

> > > > > > > *Sus.* Absurd!

Salt. You don't believe then ?

> > > > > *Sus.* A question for me!
You forget I am a double L. D.
I believe, Mr. Salt, in all that I see.
All the rest,
That will not admit of this ocular test,
Mental or real, is — fiddlededee.

Salt. Some years now gone,
Your great fool of a credulous town
Got raving Irish-mad with joy,
Because John Bull with your townsman's aid,
For his people's sake and not your own,
Beneath the ocean a means had laid
To make by a flash his two shores as one
And some day work to your annoy.
Do you doubt the flash ?   Well, you see it not.

Sus. But I know its result.

> > > > *Salt.* And as much might be said
Of the visit of ghosts to this spot.
But my friends will do more.
You shall not only hear as the media do
The ghosts of the dead, but shall see them too,
As Saul did priest Samuel's of yore.

Sus. Do you deal with the Devil ?

> > > > *Salt.* No; don't you see
How vers'd I am in Scripture lore ?

It is the Devil who deals with me.

Sus. Don't take me for one you can play your tricks on,

 Like Ferdinand Mendez Pinto Dixon,

 Who found the female American nation,

 On a single married *lady's* confession,

 Committing puerperal repression [10]

 By philosophical calculation,

 And because his apples were munch'd by one,

 Who found them more succulent than her own,

 Wish'd, for them all, that he might imbue 'em

 With the moral meaning of *meum* and *tuum.*

Salt. I see you can tell the truth sometimes.

Sus. When it does n't jar with my vocation,

 And thereby diminish the dollars and dimes.

 But what is that to our present relation?

 You would have me believe I can see without eyes.

Salt. Let not that surprise.

 How do you know that you see at all?

 How many are with me here?

      Sus. Why, two.

 No, Mr. Brim has slipp'd from view.

Brim. Bah! I am here all the while, nor so small

 But that you might see, if you really saw.

Sus. Then you stepp'd behind your fellow.

      Brim. Nor that

 Not the toe of my boots nor the crown of my hat,

 The hairs on my chin, nor the tips of my paw.

Sus. Then you are the Devil.

     Brim. I never bore

My swallow-tail'd pennant yet so high
As the great three-decker who was of yore
The Lord High Admiral of the sky.
I may be though a devil for aught you know.
But that is nothing to you, I trow,
So that we pay the debt we owe
And make you see what you doubted before.

Sus. And keep your promise ?

      Salt. What else ? Your head
Shall be a more than nine days' wonder,
And men who pay no regard to thunder
Shall do it reverence instead.

.Sus. Before I die ?

     Salt. And after too.
No man, as I said,
Nor of the living nor of the dead,
Shall prick up his ears as high as you.

Sus. But say, Mr. Salt, when shall this be?
Say where ? O where? that I shall see
That new-fangled tail to my double degree
Which shall lift me up ——

     Salt. Asinauricularly ——

Sus. With my ears prick'd up
Like a terrier-pup ——

Salt. But longer ——

    Sus. In perpetuity.

Salt. Ay, when the Griswolds and Duyckincks are rotten,
And all you have squirted yourself is forgotten,
Save one divine article

Of which not a particle
Shall be lost to the last of the Yankees begotten,[20]
Your name and your ears
Shall escape the old shears
Which, with rhymsters, is set to the thread of man's years,
And your skull shall as now be begetter of jeers
When its insides are out like a herring's that 's shotten.

Sus. O delight! O the joy! O dearest of dears,
O Salty, say when is this prospect to be?

Salt. When it suits you to talk less and trot after me.

Sus. And where? Say where!

Salt. On the other side of Slanghouse-Square;
Where Anicula's lasses
Soft-soap the asses,
And do for the masses
Other journalistic drudgery.

Sus. But we shall be seen.

Salt. What matters? She was our go-between.
Would you have your glory unnoted, unknown?

Sus. Set on!
With all your combustible matter in one.
Though all three were ramm'd,
Brimstone, Saltpeter and Charcoal, together—
It don't suit the jaws
Of a Doctor of Laws
To swear — but I 'm d — d
If I 'd mind your blow-up more than that of a feather.
Set on! set on!
With you, gunpowder three,

Or with you alone,
Mr. Salt, I 'll see,
This night, this fun.
Be it ghost or devil,
Or both or one,
To-night I 'll revel
In the feast of my fame,
Or may my short name
Still shorter be
Of its single A.M. and its double L.D.,
On the front backside of my Quarterly.
Charge, Brimstone, *charge! on*, Charcoal, *on*
To the Devil, or victory!

*Kicks over an astonished bootblack,
and Exit in a fit of enthusiasm,
followed by the three with various gestures of
admiration.*

ACT THE FIFTH

SCENE.   *Anicula's Sanctum, as in Act II.*

SALTPETER.   CHARCOAL.   BRIMSTONE.

Brim. What keeps the fool ?
                  Salt. Our LL.D. ?
Brim. The Lord of the *Ethnical Quarterly.*
Salt. In his haste to reach the rendezvous,
     The goose fell foul of an apple-wench,
     Upset her pippins, herself and bench,
     And got for himself in the kennel a drench
     Of the savory stew
     The Hotchpotian Irish corporation
     Keep mix'd for the people's delectation,
     But which to the nostrils of me and you,
     Who are us'd to the ashes and sulphurous smell
     That thicken the air round the craters of Hell
     Where the fires burn blue,
     Is a damnable abomination.
     So, holding my nose, I left him there,
     Lock'd in the claws of the dirt-mobled fair,
     Both kicking and swearing,
     And each other's clothes tearing,
     Two human beasts in a worse than beast's lair.

Brim. I suppose we shall have to await his cleaning ?

Salt. By Lucifer! yes, he will need repair

    After his pomologic careening.

    He is well pay'd already with kitchen-pitch,

    Both body and breech,

    And will get of calking more than he lists

    · From the iron fingers and mallet fists

    Of the shipwright he dubb'd an Hibernian bitch.

Brim. When he rights on his keel and floats in here,

    We will rig him with standing and running gear

    In such a wise ——

Char. His bowsprit at least,

    With its figurehead beast ——

Brim. As will make old seamen blast their eyes.

Salt. We shall give him his desert, in sooth.

    And here a contradiction lies :

    We have punish'd the bard for telling truth,

    The true in art, and in morals true,

    And now we shall make the critic rue

    His false instruction and peddling lies.

Brim. But lo, where he comes !

Enter Sus.

          Salt. What has kept you so long?

Sus. The hussy was strong.

    Before I cut loose

    From her kedge in the gutter

    The bloody Philistin,

With her great raw-meat fist in
My joles, while I utter,
In distraction, a volley of tragic abuse, —
And that not in Latin,
Though the slang came quite pat in,
From my quarterly use, —
The uncircumcis'd jade ——

Salt. Uncircumcis'd?

        Sus. Ay. Don't balk my narration.

— Demands to be paid —
Judge my rage, consternation!
For her codlings that swim — not in buttery juice.
Was *I* not too coddled? and in the same stuff?
'T was a shame! 't was a fraud! But afraid of the trollop,
Who continu'd to wollop
About me and made the mob jolly enough,
I agreed, when half-deafen'd, and after ado,
To take for five nickels the nastiest two,
Then *skedaddled*, [21] got wash'd, and came limping to you.

Salt. 'T was a Red-sea escape. · You 're a Sampson, 't is plain.

Brim. With an ass's jawbone.

        Sus. Do not talk in that strain:

I 've no wish to be vain:
One Philistine like her, though, might count for a twain.
But you, Mr. Salt, are a nice friend in need!

Salt. Why, what could I do?

There were just of you two.
I thought you well pitted;
And as you were fitted ——

Sus. You left me to bleed!

  Humph!   Let us proceed.

Salt. We are ready.   Behold!

  The blinds are down-roll'd.

Sus. And the candle burns blue.

  The devil!

    Salt. Not yet.

  He 'll not tread the scene till you get in his debt,

  Though the flame has his hue.

Sus. Do turn on the gas, Mr. Salty, please do.

Salt. Doctor dear, do not fret.

  When our drama is through,

  And your glory completed, then light up the jet.

  In this dimness the ghosts will come better in view.

Sus. Ghosts!   Oh, dear me! where 's Anicula then?

Brim. She has crawl'd back into her inner den

  To get her girls prudently out of the way.

  The dame fain would stay,

  Being jealous, and anxious to share in your glory,

  And go down like you with great ears in men's story;

  But we knew your ambition, and taught her she bare

  Length enough in her own without clipping your pair.

  But she soon will be back, I will venture to say,

  From her eagerness in the affair.

Sus. Out on the jade!   Such conduct sickens,

  As much as the money-greed of Dickens

  Who having, after his cockney mood,

  Abus'd us by all the lies he could,

  Is coming here for our Yankee pelf.

To make a greater ass of himself,

While we, like spaniels well broke-in,

Forget his thumps and vulgar curses,

And opening, like our hearts, our purses,

Beg him to help himself to our tin,

Then turn up our rumps

For more of his thumps,

And lick his toes till the kicks begin.

Salt. Eh, *Legum Doctor !* say you so ?

That is truth again.   Why, you advance !

He has not engag'd you, I see, to enhance

His low grimaces ?

           Sus. Who, Dickens ?   No.

The daily press are made fat instead,

As they always are when such feasts are spread.

We of the quarterlies sit too far

From the end of the board where the Flunkies **are,**

To come in for a share of the broken bread.

But let us begin.

Salt. Ere the dame comes in ?

With all my heart.

BRIMSTONE *disappears, and arises an Apparition.*

           What see you there?

Sus. With the large sad eyes and the youthful hair ?

His cheeks are pale and gaunt.   But what

Means here and there that discolor'd spot?

Salt. 'T is the livid mark of the poison he took ;

The sole post-obit in his look.

Sus. O, I understand; and I know him wholly.

No wonder he looks so rantipolly.

'T is the ghost, by Jove, of Thomas Rowley!

Salt. But hist, till he speaks. If he leave in disdain,

My friends may not waken him up again.

Appar. Great Master of Asses and LL.D.,

What had I done that you libel'd me?

Sus. 'T is Brimstone's voice. But the ghost is well-bred.

I see they have manners among the dead.

Libel'd! I wrote in a laud-sounding strain.

There is no "Shakspearian scholar" more hot

In the love of his idol's most whimsical blunder,

Or who takes his worst gong-beat for genuine thunder,

Than I when resounding your praises, God wot.

Appar. 'T is of that I complain.

Gapes there ever a fool

Who is fresh from the rhetoric benches at school,

But knows what sort of stuff you quote, —

Although it was not all stuff I wrote?

Is that the drama? And such its style?

You have taught your readers to stare, or smile.

That is not nature as now I know it,

And praising my verses you damn'd the poet.

Ghost vanishes, and reappears BRIMSTONE.

Sus. You are here again! Do you juggle so?

Brim. I but saw him down; which was right you know,

Since I tickled him up from his snooze below.

Sus. Oh ho!

Salt. Close up, old pup;

Another poet is sailing up.

Exit CHARCOAL, *and Apparition rises.*

Sus. His brick-red curls are sprinkled with snow.

His light eyes beam

With self-conceit, and a pleasant gleam

That is not the flash of the tragic storm.

And yet I would swear that lofty form,

With its lively face and expanded brow,

Is one I know, or ought to know.

Appar. Me, thou impertinent! know me, thou!

Thou mayst have sense in thy degree ——

Sus. In my double degree.

         Appar. Peace, vain fool!

Who thought of thy honors from college or school?

Despite thy A.M. ——

         Sus. And my double L. D.

Appar. Thou mayst have line enough to gage

The shoal still pool, where no tempests rage,

Of *the Spanish Student*, or measure *Queechy*,

Not the depths of *Filippo* or *Polini"ce*.

Sus. That terrible voice is Charcoal's own,

Though ten times louder, and haughty in tone.

I know him now, with his scalp so hairy

And whiskerless jaws. It is Count Alfieri.

     VOL. IV.—20

Appar. *Count* unto thee, whose envious hate
  Reproach'd me with pride in that titled lot
  Which by right of birth so natural sate
  On my father's name that I felt it not;
  But to the world my works still bore
  Victor Alfieri, and nothing more:
  A pride by you not understood,
  Who have stuck the letters of both your degrees,
  Cheap and unearn'd although they were ——
Sus. To that I demur;
  I paid for them twenty ——

      Appar. Silence, cur! —
  Have thrust each cheap, unearn'd degree,
  That men your sole claims to knowledge might see,
  On every side, wherever you could ——
Sus. No, Signor Contè, if you please,
  On the bare backside of my Quarterly,
  And with some of the Press, in notice or puff,
  Whom I patronize for a *quantum suff.*
  We do all things here for cash you know, —
  Though you go on tick, I suppose, below.
Appar. Silence, once more! —   That thou hast try'd,
  Thou to whom honor nor truth is known,
  To asperse my fame, who liv'd and dy'd
  Slave unto Truth, and Truth alone,
  This I forgive, though thou shalt atone
  To that public judgment thou hast defy'd.
Sus. Have mercy, good ghost, nor deprive me of bread:
  In my next I will take back all I have said, —

On the word of a critic, and as sure as you 're dead!

Appar. Hound! dar'st thou deem I am like thy tribe,

To cant or recant as men pay or bribe ?

Thy aspersions are praise, and another pen

Shall make of them mirth for the gizzards of men.

But what I can neither forgive nor forget,

Until in the regions above I am set

Where men o'er their wrongs are not suffer'd to fret ——

Sus. And no Minor critics condemn in a pet.

Appar. A pest on thy pestilent tongue! — What is worse,

I say, than thy praise, thou hast made me rehearse

As I never yet spoke, nor in prose nor in verse.

Unasham'd thou hast ventur'd to strip off the buskin

From the feet of my toga'd and chlamydate Tuscan,

And clap on the socks of thy English instead,

Slipshod, and soft as the pap of thy head.

Better in tinsel, cross-garter'd, to tread

With the stage-strut of Emerson, Carlyle and Ruskin.

Sus. *Peccavi! sed non mea culpa ;* not mine

The soft worsted ; I bought it at sixpence a line.

The all that I did was to lend it some picking :

I adopted the cub ; but I gave him a licking.

Appar. Didst thou so ? Now I 'm minded to give thee a
kicking.

But the weakness or want of the flesh has come o'er me,

And Brimstone and Charcoal must do the job for me.

Apparition vanishes, and reappears CHARCOAL.

Sus. He has *vamos'd the ranch.*[22]   And there 's Charcoal again!

This is all hocuspocus, or masking; that 's plain.

Char. Not a whit. Do you think a sixfooter like him

   Could step from his niche in the Shades, nor be miss'd?

Sus. Why, the chance were but slim.

Char. — So I took up his place in Probational Hell,

   And escap'd all detection by means of its mist.

   As for masking, how could a paste-board imitation

   Be proof to the lens of your us'd penetration?

Sus. Very right, Mr. Coal. Vain to hope it. As well

   Look for judgment in Greeley, or truth in the *Nation*,

   Bid Raymond stand still for a minute, or Sedley

   Tell more than he hides in his fortnightly medley.

Salt. What are those? Of the four, are unknown to me three.

Sus. One a coverless journal; the others are asses,

   That mix, though unlike, as do milk and molasses,

   And wake pity and mirth when they bray to the masses,

   Like the *Ethnos* or me.

Salt. My friends now, great Doctor, have shown you their
   power:

   I have kept half my word; you know how ghosts look.

   Will it do? Shall they summon up more? But the hour

   Is late, and the dame will be leaving her nook.

Sus. No, give me the rest of your promise; I long

   To wear my grand ears and be famous in song.

Salt. It is well: but not yet. You have shown yourself brave.

   You are leag'd hand and glove with the servants of
   Hell —

Sus. Not with you? [*in alarm.*

            Salt. Never mind. — And chop logic as well

With the pupæ whose sordid cocoon is the grave.

By these two acts alone,

Already you wear them.

But forever to bear them

And by them be known,

You must prove by your gifts they are truly your own.

Sus. By my gifts? How you prate! Am I not LL.D.,

And was A.M. before?

Then give them to me.

By the Powers ye adore,

By the shame I defy

Were it doubled twice o'er,

O Saltpeter, I cry,

Let me feel, ere I die,

My long ears stand up somewhat nearer the sky!

Salt. Can you go through the proofs that shall make these gifts

known?

Sus. Through them all! Only try.

Salt. O hero!

     Sus. Be quick!

          Salt. On thy four paws go down.

And give him the halter. What! up? So soon scar'd?

Sus. I would hang for the ears; but my neck must be spar'd.

Neck or nothing.

       Salt. With us, it is nothing indeed.

To know you have patience, can keep your own way

Spite of coaxing or curses —

Save when flatter'd your greed

Is by dreams of full purses —

Nor, shamefac'd, will heed
The worst men may say,
This is all that we need.

Sus. That exception observ'd, which is wise nowadays
When a patron is valu'd for what he disburses,
The rest is as light as to spawn tadpole verses
Such as *Round-Robins* praise,
While Fledgling, who knows not which most to admire,
A jewsharp, or bagpipe, or Æolus' lyre,
But dotes on Walt Whitman's batrachian fire,[23]
Shall, in love with their long tails, the porwiggles feed
As full-breech'd green frogs of the Horse-fountain breed.

Salt. What! what! truth again? If you sing in this strain,
  Your ears will be stretch'd to the ass point in vain.

Sus. Never fear: I but stumble thus trotting alone,
Or with friends; in my journal I rein-in my roan,
And decide by my belly and not by my brains.

Salt. True metal! But quick; on your quarters once more.
How the halter becomes him! Now clap on the pack.
While Charcoal sits woman-wise perch'd on his back,
You, Brim, jerk his tail, while I drag him before.

Sus. But don't jerk so hard, or my tail will be torn.
'T is my best workday-coat and is only half-worn.
And don't kick so much. Ow! ow!

                              Salt. If you cry,
You 'll have more than the dame bouncing in to know why.

Sus. O my! O my!
O my seat of honor!
Pray, don't spank so hard! The dame — curse upon her!

Let me up! let me up!   The dame — d—n the wench!
She sha' n't see me stretch'd like a washermaid's bench.

Salt. Do you pull up so soon ?

      Sus. Up?   'T is you beat me down.
My rump 's not an ass's, whatever my crown.

Salt. But the ears?

     Sus. Let them go.   Ow! I 'm beat black and blue. ✓
I can't carry Charcoal and bear your kicks too.

Salt. Let him rise.   It will do.

Sus. Do ? my back 's almost broken.

Salt. You have prov'd it of steel.

 And this is the token :

 You have kept your own way

 Like a genuine ass, — though with rather more bray.

Sus. But, for all that, I feel.

 Now give me the ears.

     Salt. Not as yet.   You have shown,
 It is true, soul and carcass, an ass's backbone.

 You must now make it known

 You can swing to the popular breath of the nation,

 And to private dictation —

Sus. For a gratification —

Salt. To and fro with a prompt oscillation,

 Or round with a gallowsbird's circumgyration,

 Whatever the compass-point whence it is blown.

Sus. Pshaw! I do that with ease!   Not Weathercock Flunky,

 Though daily, more duly, nor his Topical monkey.

Salt. Let us see!   Hang him up by his weasand.

      Sus. [*in alarm.*] What 's that!

I will not box the compass — sâve on paper, — that's flat!

Salt. But you must, or no ears.   Fix the hook.   Trice him up.
   By the coat-collar only, you ninny.

                              Sus. You 'll tear it.

Salt. But the glory, the ears!   Will you lose them, to spare it?

Sus. O me! I shall dangle just like a blind pup.

Salt. Or a sheep in the shambles.

                       Sus. But whence come these things;
   The hoop, and the ring in the ceiling, and block,
   With the rope that thence swings?

Salt. They are brought by the phantoms on tables that knock.

Sus. Pheew!

       Salt. What, doubting?   'T is harder to hurl fiddles
       round
   On the sconces of gazers and make guitars sound
   By invisible thumbs, as your Davenports do.

Sus. That is true.

Salt. As the ghosts of the verse-men we summon'd to view.
   There.   Up with him! oo!

Sus. Oh, oh! let me down!   Let me down, or I 'll cry!
   My brains are aswound.
   My heels kiss the ceiling
   And my skull treads the ground.
   I don't know which is which while my brainpan keeps
       reeling
   And my navel goes round.

                       They unhook him.

Salt. So.   You have learn'd vacillation.

Sus. I knew it of yore,

While you slabber'd your mother, or even I trow
Were coil'd up a *fœtus in utero,*
To your daddy's delectation.

Salt. You practic'd then shifting, some ages or more
Ere the Spirit that brooding sat over the deep
Put the breathing red clay in his consciousless sleep,
To produce an equivocal first generation.

Sus. Oh horror! I 'm hous'd with the Father of Sin,
Or one of his kin.

Salt. With neither. But what if you were, so you win?
Set your heart on the ears,
And your feet on these fears;
Your fame shall grow younger while olden the years.

Sus. Enough. Shall I more? Through the Devil and Hell
I would stride to my glory. Push onward.

Salt. 'T is well.

You must next learn false candor.

Sus. I avow that in that

Round Robin 's my master.

Salt. He needs not to be.

You have only to hide what is lofty as he,
And vaunt to the skies the ignoble or flat.

Sus. I do! I do!
Witness your ghosts if I do not speak true?

Salt. But to make that appear,
You must perch on your head with your claws in the air.

Sus. O spare! O spare!
Set me down, set me down!
All the blood leaves my seat to descend to my crown.
20*

Set me down, or I 'm dead:

My brain is afire, my eyes flame ; I 'm sped !

O my soul !

Salt. [*righting him.*

You are all over red.

'T is the dawn of your triumph.

Sus. No, the set of my pole.

I hope this is all.

    Salt. Not enough for your fame.

The next thing to learn is the goodbye to shame.

Sus. I have bid it already.   Attest that, my Quarterly.

Not inside alone, but without, as you ought to see,

It is printed in full.

     Salt. Where your name is.   We know it.

But off with your breeches, and caper to show it.

Sus. There.

Brim, let them down tenderly, else they will tear.

Ye gods, I am bare !

Salt. Let us chant.

    Sus. Well, begin.

Salt. Now, Doctor, keep time.

     Sus. And, in time, if the air

Suit my taste, I 'll chime in.

   Salt. *In puris naturalibus,*

    The Doctor's dainty legs discuss

    The lines of beauty, capering thus,

    As if he 'd pass'd at Willis'.[24]

Sus. The air however 's rather cool.
    I think you make me play the fool,
    Too plump for nature's dancingschool,
    With short *tendo Achillis.*

Brim. Give him a kick, to spin him round;
Char. Another, for the pair that 's found
    Of cushions waiting their rebound.
Salt. But spring a little higher.

Sus. I would the world could see my shame,
    Who caper thus for future fame —
Salt. As David, when he 'd won the game
    Of Jack-stones with Goliah.

Sus. Yet stop! though dancing does agree
    With naked tibial dignity,
    It hardly suits my Quarterly,
    Although it saves my breeches.

    Besides, my breath is growing short.
Salt. And, Doctor, you have made good sport,
    A Sampson in Philistine court,
    As *Judges* XV. teaches.

Sus. How well you know the sacred text!
Salt. It is my forte; and Henry Beecher
    Himself might be perhaps perplex'd,

Although a most accomplish'd preacher,
To follow where my memory reaches,
And think perhaps that Satan preaches.

Sus. He often does, rude laics say.
I have known myself a broker pray,
And cheat his client the same day
And bring him to the verge of starving,
Say grace to his thanksgiving-dinner,
(His creditor had none, mean sinner !)
Then smile, as doubtless should the winner,
The while a sumptuous sirloin carving.
But have I done ?

    Salt. We pause, you see.

Char. First, accept these two love spanks,
Given, if with emotion rough,
One on each cheek, yet tenderly.

Sus. One for both were caress enough.
Yet for the gift I render thanks.

Char. And ought, for your hide is beastly tough.

Sus. 'T is sitting so long at my task ev'ry quarter.
'T would harden the beef of an alderman's daughter.

Char. Or of Brimstone, or me.

Sus. I have danc'd and sung, and I feel ecstatic
From fundament to Mansard attic.
I would there were no more to do,
Than shake a leg with Salt and you.
But help me now my drawers induc :
Their want gives over much to view,
And makes me seem erratic.

I only wish the dullard crew,
Who make pretensions to review
The poets they can scarcely read,
Would dance like me in cuerpo once
'T would fire the liver of each dunce,
And, acting on his brain-pulp, serve
To make him guess at tragic verve.
Please hold my drawers awhile, while now
I wipe the dewdrops from my brow
Of wholesome perspiration.
I do not like to swear, yet vow,
With shirt and jacket on and coat,
Cravatted too, but *sans culotte*,
I 'm like the bird that talks by rote
Bi-monthly in *the Nation*.
Come, give the calicos.

    Salt. Not yet.
As 't is convenient, let us set
His titles on his naked parts,
Laws' Doctor and great man of Arts.

Sus. M. stands for Master, not Man, Mister.

Char. So brand it *Artium Magister*.
  Bring the iron that sears.

Sus. No, no! by my tears!
  Make me not a freemason — at least not for life!
  If the brand should be seen! —— Have regard for my
    wife.

Salt. He has suffer'd enough,
  And has prov'd the right stuff.

Let us give him the ears.

Sus. O joy !

    Salt. Hold your tongue : it is greatly too long.

Sus. And a long tongue licks up vexation.

    You forget my degrees and might have spar'd me the wrong

    Of that vocative mortification.

Salt. Well, hush then, great Doctor, and listen the song, —

    While you, Brimstone and Charcoal,

    Stop with spittle each earhole,

    And rub up, nor mind the pain ——

Sus. Yes, yes ; for mine the pain.

Salt. — The rims, till they shine again, —

    The song of our Incantation.

    But first, though you have prov'd a wonder

    In bestial worth, and may defy

    Compare, yet this is to supply :

    You must tread conscience wholly under,

    Boldly dash and never blunder,

    Ere your ears will reach the sky.

Sus. Then crown the work, nor more deny

    My honors ; nought is to be fear'd ;

    My conscience is already Scar'd.

    Save Deadhead sole and Flunky's Fledgling,

    I know not any moral ridgling

    Can sense and decency defy,

    Suppress the truth, or boldly lie,

    With such indifference as I.

Salt. Well then, attend ; and while Coaly and Brim

    Bespittle your holes and chafe each ear-rim,

Make no outcry.

INCANTATION.

By the spirits in darkness dwelling,
Styebak'd, half-naked, and wholly obscene;
By the thick oils from underground welling,
Making naptha and kerosene; —

Sus. What a queer charm!
Salt. If you 'd not come to harm,
You will take good care not to cross my spelling.

By the sheet-lightning, that dazzles, not kills,
Image of force that is only in seeming;
By the miasms from stagnant pools steaming,
Filling men's vitals with fever and chills;

By the town-council in mud that reposes,
Shellfish that neither are oyster nor clam,
By their vile gutters that reek not of reses,
Making the taxpayers frown, spit and damn;

Sus. And press hard their noses.
Salt. Will you hold?
Sus. Having roll'd
But just now in that clover,
I have study'd its botany over and over,
And thought I might add, as a note, 'T is no sham.
But be quick; for my auricles are glowing;

And my digits can't find out at all that they 're growing.
Salt. Patience and list.   When the charm is all sung.
  Your ears will have almost the stretch of your tongue.

        By all that is vile, or in nothingness ending,
        Borrow'd and full of pretension vain,
        Come with your tails up, straight, corkscrew'd, and
            bending,
        Creatures that symbol his heart and his brain:

        Monkey and magotpie, paddock and frog,
        And spitting she-kitten and snarling cur-dog,
        Reremouse, and nyctalopic owl,
        Crocodile grim, and hyena fowl, —
        His arts' eido'la and types of his mind,
        Surround him, caress him; he is of your kind.

Sus. O me! O me!   I wish I was blind.
    The owl 's on my head.
    And the monkey —— You imp, take your paws off!
        Let go;
    Or you 'll strangle me.   Oh!
    And that beast from the Nile,
    With his amplify'd smile,
    His yard-long mouth — scissors and chopper and file,
    Keep him back, or I 'm dead.
Salt. O fi! O fi!
    A Doctor, and cry?

These spirits, though evil,
Will give health to your navel,
Not make you to die.
They will teach you to mimic, — to prate without mean-
ing, —
To stare without seeing, — to puff without pride, —
To feign frozen chastity,
While in hot nastity
Seeking by harsh words lust-itching to hide, —
To growl o'er the stript bones you're savagely cleaning, —
To tear from their graves and disfigure the dead, —
To be daz'd with the twilight,
Half mouse and half sparrow,
And dash, like an arrow
Misshot, through a skylight, —
To croak with facility
The tuneless un-sense of a sapless anility, —
And give you ability
By a shrewd crocodility
To make shoddy seem broadcloth in all you have said.
In fine, they will stuff, with goëtic agility,
Your brainpot with feathers and your heart's pipes with
lead.

Sus. The dear ugly creatures! Each fright is a fairy.
I feel my ears prick, my os frontis grows hairy.
O Stoney, O dear Coal,
Spit your best at each ear-hole,
Nor of friction be chary.
O feathers and lead!

Ah feathers and lead!

You were wrong, noble Salty, in what you last said:

My head 't is grows heavy, my heart that is airy.

O, O!

I wish I could show

My crown to all Hotchpot at once.   Let me go.

But the phantoms are leaving.   Goodbye, my dear
    creatures.

The valves of my heart shall shut-in your sweet features;

Especially yours, armor'd Earl of the Nile,

With your skillet-handle tail and your waffle-iron smile.

Adieu! adieu! —

Now, my rubbers, to you,

Whose hands have the magic of Moses,

I turn and demand,

Is there aught in this land

Can compare with my metamorpho'sis?

Char. It is all very well; a good head of its kind.

Sus. Good?   'T is complete in each elegant feature,

    And fits me like a second nature.

Char. And there is the very fault I find:

    'T is too natural far.

    It makes you appear,

    Jaws, forepiece and ear,

    Without counting the hair,

    Like the ass that you are.

Sus. Say, donkey: it fits not my bifold degree

    To be nam'd, though mark'd, asinauricularly.

    But seem I the same?

And if I be known by that recogniz'd name,
Which is Fledgling's and Deadhead's
And some other leadheads',
I who have run the whole college curriculum,
Why what upon earth shall cognominate me ?

Char. Asinor'um Magis'ter, Lectōrum' Deridic'ulum.

Sus. Why, that is my A.M. and double L. D. !
But here is Anicula.   Now we shall see.

Enter ANICULA.

Anic. Eh !   Bottom the weaver !
Now, would I were Titania for thy sake.
I 'd "kiss thy fair large ears, my gentle joy."

Sus. Dost think I 'd hug a doxy of your make ?
I would as soon buss Fledgling, or a boy.
But oh thou deceiver ! [*gaily to Salt.*
If one may believe her,
Who 's as false as *the Nation*,
She at least, 't would appear,
Is fully aware
Of my beautiful transfiguration.
For this I adore thee,
And could kneel down before thee,
And aye ready to serve am.

Anic. Sure, 't is old Sus Minervam !
That fools-voice reveal'd him,
As the dim light conceal'd him.
Pray, let me explore thee.

Why, you 're perfect, I vow.
Feels it good?

   Sus. Bless the maker,

'T is my soul's simulachre :

I never had justice till now.

Anic. Mr. Salt, give me one, —

 But your candle burns dim.

Salt. Ancient dame, you need none. —

 Light the gas, Mr. Brim.

Sus. He does 't with his fingers ! Is the devil in him?

Salt. No, on my veracity,

 'T is his Brimstone capacity.

 He has the felicity

 To use electricity

 Like matches, for fun.

Anic. But again for the ass-head. Why don't I need one?

Salt. It would make you less trim.

 And, as simple Anicula,

 In your function particular

 You give quite as droll delectation,

 By your senile garrulity

 And anile credulity ——

Sus. As if you were chief of *the Nation.*

 But here come two witlings, to heighten my joy, —

 Though one is a monkey ;

 Polyphemus's boy

 And the turnspit of Flunky.

 I 'll play mum and enjoy their surprise.

Enter DEADHEAD *and* FLEDGLING.

Dead. Old lady, your humble contumble.   My eyes!
  What a mask!
        Fledg. And what size!
  I will make on 't a note for my *Topics*.
  We don't breed such at home.
  Whence can the beast come?
Dead. From Aspis, I think, in the Tropics.
  Anic', you she-monkey,
  Get on the old donkey.
Sus. No you don't.
        Fledg. Eh! 't is Sus.
  Who gave him those ears?
Anic. Mr. Salt, it appears;
  Or, it may be, the Devil.
Fledg. Fi, old woman, be civil.
  Give them, wise man, to us.
Sus. Be off, and don't trouble him.
  They are mine, and mine only.
Salt. Fear not, I can't double them;
  Though, your asshead's not lonely.
Fledg. Can we make no conditions?   I feel we shall die,
  If outdone by the Doctor, Mort-Caput and I.
Anic. What stuff!   Don't I stand in my petticoat by?
Sus. Well protested, old dame of the *Ethnos;* but higher
  Than greatness soars envy, as smoke above fire.
Salt. Notwithstanding, these witlings shall have their desire.
Fledg. How?

Dead. Say how !

Salt. By leaving your birth-marks to stand just as now ;
    Only making each feature
    Better photograph nature,
    As with the great Doctor, on jaw, nose and brow.

Dead. Begin then, begin.

Fledg. But is it not sin ?

Dead. Out, sanctity !   Is n't there money to win ?
    Push on, jolly proctor,
    Make us grin like the Doctor,
    We 'll line you with greenbacks or plate you with tin.

Salt. Attend then.

        Sus. *Fave'te.*

        Fledg. That means, Stop your din.

Salt. Not from the spirit-world need we to summon
    Biped or quadruped, feathers or hair,
    Haunting stream, standing-pool, cockloft or common,
    From their mud, hole or perch, kennel or lair.

    Take   these   two   newspapers,   wet   with   men's
    water ——

Anic. Of my girl's making, nevertheless.

    Salt. Mind not the ancient dame; envy has taught
    her ——

Anic. Knowledge of earthenware, rather confess.

Salt. Clap them upon your head, occiput, sinciput —

Anic. But do it tenderly, else they will tear.

Sus. They 're your own daily sheets.   Mind not the stingy slut.

Salt. Press them to mouth and nose, eyelids and hair.

Dead. But they are devilish salt.
Salt. That 's not the devil's fault.
Fledg. No, 't is humanity's.
                  Anic. That you may swear.

Salt. As in the *Hours'* page flatness and fickleness,
      Laughable graveness and mawkish mirth meet;
      As in the *Cryer* mere spluttering words express
      All that 's not ribald or worse in its sheet;

      So shall these papers impress on your faces
      Types of each soul's inward birth-given shape,
      Make Deadhead a parrot, give you the grimaces,
      The solemn inaneness and mirth of an ape.

It is done.   Lift the sheet;
The impression 's complete.

Dead. I am glad; for the print 's too much stal'd to be sweet.

Anic. Eh, the trio! How fine!

Sus. But my asshead 's the best.

Anic. And I alone left, all unchang'd!

                 . *Sus.* Don't be vex'd.

Anic. When my virtue alone in the group 's unexpress'd?

    I were better unsex'd.

Salt. You need not repine:

    You attract as much note

    By your petticoat.

Fledg. And are free of the brine.

Dead. A parrot, a monkey, an ass and old maid.

    Let us get up a dance for our masquerade.

Fledg. But where is the music?

                 Salt. Behold, to your aid.

Fledg. The fiddle, the bones and the banjo already!

    I fear that the Devil is piper.

                  Salt. Not he.

Sus. They come from the spirits.

                 Salt. No matter; keep steady:

    You *may* have the Devil to pay, but not me.

Sus. That is something; I like contributions post-free.

Fledg. But, Doctor, turn in.

               Sus. I am fagg'd. Ere you came,

    I danc'd a long Indian pas-seul for my fame,

    And toe'd it unbreech'd, proof to cold and to shame.

Dead. Then you 've practice; a male Taglioni. Fall in.

    Scrape up now, good catgut, and let us begin.

Fledg. Up and down, and in and out,
    Chassez, promenez round about.
Dead. It is better-leg-shaking, than pens, no doubt.
    Fol de rol!

Sus. The one is hard shuffling, the other mere play.
    No donkey could stand that, except for pay.
Fledg. You mean, I suppose, for thistles or hay.
Sus. It is one. And an ass cannot always bray
    Without pause in his vocalization.

Dead. And a parrot must swing, as well as talk.
Fledg. And a monkey won't always on two legs walk.
Anic. Nor a petticoat either swap cheese for chalk,
    Who is not in a situation.
Sus. Except ——
    Dead. But, Doctor, keep time; you balk.
Sus. — For a handsome consid-e-ration.
Dead. Fol de rol.

Fledg. Cross over. Ladies change. You see,
    We beat the devils in *Calvary.*
Dead. That is easy; they danc'd without fiddle-de-dee
    Fol de lol.

Fledg. Balance. I never had so much fun,
    Except when I found an author done.
Dead. Or the public diddled.
        Anic. It is all one,

In our soi-disant critical function.

Fledg. To cog, dissemble, misrepresent;
　　　　To fool the public to its bent;
　　　　And wink when it sees what never was meant;
　　　　Is interest rich; but cent per cent ——
Sus. Is our Terpsichorean junction.

Dead. Forward two.　What a jolly dance!
Fledg. And what music! 'T would make an old donkey
　　　　prance.
Sus. Or a tailless monkey.
　　　　　　　　Fledg. Its pleasures enhance,
　　　　And with a particular zest,
　　　　The joy I had to make Tilton cry,
　　　　When I quoted as proof of his powers *The Fly.*
Dead. Well, why did n't Sheldon your blarney buy?
Fledg. Or yours?　You know, as well as I,
　　　　He may rank with New England's best.[25]

Dead. One jackass foward.　Now back again.
　　　　Now lady and ape.
　　　　　　　　Anic. Let me hold up my train.
Dead. Come, Be'lzebub, scrape us another strain.
　　　　Fol de lol.

　　　　Enter GALANTUOM, HEARTANDHEAD,
　　　　　　　and ATTICUS.

Gal. Why, what the deuse are you all about?

Sus. Do you see our heads?

     Gal. To be sure we do.

And your legs as well. You 're a jolly crew.

Few editors, even the dolts of *the Nation*,

Would after this fashion make saltation

To fiddle and flute. You caper without.

Sus. You must be stone-deaf and gravel-blind.

Don't you see our little band?

'T is of the best of the fiddling kind

To be found in all the land.

Saltpeter has now the horsehair in hand,

And Brimstone rattles the bones,

And little Charcoal'

From the banjo's hole

Is drawing those bullfrog tones.

Gal. The devil! the banjo has no hole.

Heart. He must mean "the light guitar."

Sus. No, I don't; I mean just what I say:

The banjo's bottom is all away.

Dead. And as Sambo says, *dat 's dar.* —

No matter, strike up,

My devils-bullpup,

And show them what you are.

  Fledg. Up the middle and down again.

  Dead. Sweep in, broomsticks, might and main.

  Sus. Rest for muscle is rust for brain.

  Anic. Up the middle and down again.

Att. Why, they are all four crazy !

                    Fledg. Are we so ?

    You are, all three, fools.

Dead. You are blind as new kittens, and don't seem to know

    There 's lots of pleasure in such a go.

Sus. " Dul'ce est desip'ere in loco'."

Anic. What is that ?

Dead. Some Hebrew that 's pat,

    • Fundamentally taught in the schools.

Sus. But you don't mark my ears' length, you don't note my
        head,

    Those emblems of glory to be.

    Be abash'd when you learn there lurks under this shed

    The brain of Sus, double L. D.

    Behold too that green-noddled parrot, that monkey

    Which belongs to the kind that are minus a tail:

    The first one picks grubs from the *Cryer* man's nail,

    The other is turnspit to Weathercock Flunky.

Heart. A parrot, a monkey, a head and long ears !

    This is worse than the Quarterly gabble of Sears.

Fledg. And you see not the changes ?

                    Gal. We see but three men,

    Two of whom have their faces

    Smear'd with what seems the traces

    Of types, and an elderly dame, in this den.

Sus. And you heard not the music?

                  Att. We heard upon the floor

    The shuffling of your feet and your bacchanalian roar,

    As you shambled to and fro.

Only this.

  Dead. Says Raven Poe :

" Only this, and nothing more."

Sus. And you don't then see the triad ?

        Att. What triad ?

         Sus. Our small band,

With the banjo, and the beef-bones, and the fiddle-bow in
 hand.

There they stand.

Att. Where ?

  Sus. At the wall.

Att. I see but a petticoat ——

     Dead. " Hanging to dry." [26]

Att. And an old straw bonnet by,

 And a shawl.

Sus. Then you 're crazy, else am I.

Att. To my thinking,

 It is wine.

Fledg. What the Doctor has been drinking,

 With the ancient virgin here,

 Is his own affair.

 But, I say it without shrinking,

 Save our beer,

 Dead and I have tasted nothing ——

      Dead. Only brine.

Fledg. Yet we see the ass's ear,

 And behold the triad there,

 Who have, to our delectation,

 Made this triple transformation.

That is clear.

Gal. Here 's some juggle.

                  Sus. You are crazy.

Mr. Peter, Charcoal, Brim:
Lift these skeptics' leaden-eyes.
In this room the air 's not hazy,
No more burns the candle dim;
In the gaslight ——

              Dead. Even an ass might
At your blindness show surprise.

Salt. As I hinted once before,
Strangers to your worth are blind;
And the glory of your asshood
With your friends alone will pass good,
Monkies, parrots, and such kind.
This, although 't you may deplore, —

Dead. " Quoth the Raven, Evermore," —

Salt. 'T is not in our power to alter.
Only human optics heed us
In the sconce of fools who need us,
Who with truth and conscience palter
Or are like yourself in mind.

Sus. Did you hear?

            Gal. What? Deadhead's joke?

Sus. No, that other voice which spoke.

Gal. No one else the stillness broke.

Att. We were struck to see you staring
At those rags for women's wearing,
As if pondering their repairing,

Hanging on the dingy wall.

Sus. Then the devil must be in it!

O my asshead!   And to win it,

Was 't for this I stoop'd to shin it?

Bore with kick and spank and thwack?

More, bore Charcoal on my back?

Nor that all;

Swung like smok'd meat from the ceiling,

Stood on end till brains were reeling,

And, my southern pole revealing,

Boldly let my breeches fall?

Dead. So the game is up!   We 're diddled.

'T was old Be'lzebub that fiddled.

Let 's *skedaddle*, great and small.

Salt. But before you scud, believe me,

In this mummery goëtic

There was nothing to deceive ye.

Each shall flourish still a critic,

With the traits that here he bore.

You shall be, to all who know you,

Still a parrot, and a monkey,

Mimicking and nothing more,

He who turns the spit for Flunky.

Still the ancient dame shall drape her

In old frippery and shape her

Worn head-gear to suit her paper;

While the LL.D. shall show you

All his asshead as before.

Heart. How they stare!   They are surely crazy.

Dead. No, we 're listening but; be aisy.

Sus. To a prophecy, expressing ——

Fledg. That our cake is not all dough.

Salt. Take, before you leave, this blessing.

Brim. Mine too.

   Char. Mine too, Doctor.

     Sus. Oh !

Spare ! Have mercy ! Such a basting

For my ham is more than wasting :

I 've no relish for the dressing. [*Exit — manipulating.*

Gal. Good night, Doctor.

   Dead. There 's a go !

Take more time. With so much hasting,

You may reach too soon below.

Fledg. Come, old fellows, not for us

Such rump-roasting.

   Dead. Don't stay tasting :

Let us hasten after Sus.

Fledg. D—n them, no ; pitch in.

   Dead. Our breeches

'Gainst their hoofs have slim defences.

Damn'd they are. Come, St. Paul teaches

Counter-kicking never thrives.

Sus. [*from below.*] Bring down with you, lads, my beaver. —

Take my curse, you arch deceiver !

Salt. Why ? Your asshood aye survives.

Att. Have these men not lost their senses ?

Heart. Were they ever theirs, to lose them ?

Gal. Look ! you 'd think their legs had lives.

Dead. Gad! we 've no choice but to use them.
Needs must when the devil drives.

Exeunt hastily
FLEDGLING *and* DEADHEAD,
*the former in tragic huff, and are followed
deliberately and wonderingly by*
GALANTUOM, HEARTANDHEAD *and* ATTICUS.

SALTPETER, BRIMSTONE, *and* CHARCOAL,
first lifting up ANICULA *by the petticoat, causing her to
sprawl and kick out like a toy spider, to the great damage of her
virginal modesty, convert the medical advertisements of the*
HOURS *and the* CRYER *into sulphuretted hydrogen
and ascend through the ceiling by the vapor.*

Manet
ANICULA *in dishabille,
with the blank expression of the* ETHNOS.

21*

NOTES

TO

THE SCHOOL FOR CRITICS

1.—P. 405. — *Slanghouse-Square* —] There is a place in New-York with a somewhat similar composite name, borrowed in like manner, with a ridiculous apery, from a locality in London. But in that case it is a triangle, a scalene of the most irregular proportions, and indeed amorphous, the two longest sides not meeting at all, although they converge. However, a figure of three angles for a parallelogram is as near as the journal which originated the euphonious designation can be expected to come to correctness.

2.—P. 405. — *in rogues abounding, Who draw from the public pot their fare And openly,* etc.] This is so like the kind of men which Mr. Parton gave to public admiration in the *N. American Review*, that, were it not for the name of the city, one might suppose they sat for the outline in New York. But as no individual is whatever his pre-eminence, absolutely singular, so it may be that every corporation has, however monstrous its rascality, somewhere its congeners.

3.—P. 406. *That is why, one day, To get appointed,* etc.] This is one of the bad features of our popular government, the nomination to high office of members of the Press. Supposing they were equally well-qualified as certain others, — which is taking a very great deal on assumption, — yet the office serves as a bribe, and the influence of a widely circulating newspaper is cheaply bought at any price by the candidate for election or re-election to the Presidency. The corruption thus produced on both sides, in the relation of cause and effect, needs not to be demonstrated.

4.—P. 408. *And stirring up rubbish he cry'd, " Oh fine !"*] It was not to be expected that any professional critic would presume to attack an author of established reputation, far less that those who know nothing of literary criticism but its pretension should be able to discriminate between the false and the true ; but that such an exhibition of absurdity should be made in any journal of standing as is paraded, with full trumpet-accompaniment, in the following passage of the *N. Y. Times* of May 18, 1867, would be incredible except to those familiar with its sycophancy in letters, or who know by experience its ignorance therein and absolute indifference to principle.

" Sometimes too, it would seem that Mr. Longfellow's exceeding familiarity with the Italian, and his unswerving attention to its literal signification leads [lead] him into obscurity. An instance of this may be found in the sixth line of canto XXIV. which Mr. Longfellow renders —

' But little lasts the temper of her pen.'

The word pen here is precisely the same as the original *penna*, but the reader who knows nothing of DANTE would be in doubt as to the meaning of the line. So in line thirty-six of the same canto :

' He I know not, but I had been dead beat.'

The last half of this line has never been equaled by any former translator."

I should think not. It is a "dead beat" altogether. Had I, or Cluvienus, used such slang — on any occasion whatever ! And for so ordinary a phrase :

" Non so di lui ; ma io sarei *ben rinto*."

The fact is, if the specimens given in the *Times* and in the *Tribune* are fair examples of Mr. Longfellow's work, it will show that his capacity as a poet is, in every respect, far below what even his most moderate admirers have allowed him. Mr. L., it may be supposed, considered, that, as Dante himself frequently uses coarse and even grotesque phrases, he was but imitating the Dantescan spirit when he introduced this vulgarism and slang of the turf or chase. If so, he transcended his part, which was to follow, not to lead, and not to libel his original by adding to his crudities. But these newspaper critics! * ——

* The *Times* goes on to cite what it calls an " incomparable picture: "

" Quivi sospiri, pianti ed alti guai
Risonavan per l'aer senza stelle,
Perch' io al cominciar ne lagrimai.
Diverse lingue, orribili favelle,
Parole di dolore, accenti d'ira,
Voci alte e fioche, e suon di man con elle,
Facevano un tumulto il qual s'aggira
Sempre 'n quell' aria senza tempo tinta,
Come la rena quando 'l turbo spira." (*Inf.* III.)

Of this it gives seven translations. The best of these is, as might be supposed, the German; but "of all the English versions," it tells us, — in the face of Mr. Wright's and Dr. Parsons', — "Mr. Longfellow's is unquestionably both the most literal and the most *poetic*.". . . Let us have it, including the two extraordinary lines here italicized:

" There sighs, complaints and ululations loud
Resounded through the air without a star.
Whence I, at the beginning, wept thereat.
Languages diverse, horrible dialects,
Accents of anger, words of agony
And voices high and hoarse, with sound of hands,
Made up a tumult that goes whirling on
Forever in that air forever black
Even as the sand doth when the whirlwind breathes."

I knew beforehand, judging from such as I have redd of Mr. Longfellow's poems, and redd (the smaller ones) with unqualified admiration, that their author was by the very character of his mind inadequate to a version of the stern and masculine Florentine, but I never could have dreamed that he would have the folly to attempt, in these days, to render him without the rhyme which is so es-

5.—P. 410. *Amen ! as said on his knees Jeff Davis*, etc.] Godliness was a characteristic trait of this eminent personage, — eminent, I mean, in virtues.   A lady of Richmond was much edified by seeing

sential to a true imitation.   But my greatest surprise has been at the translator's blank verse.   His extraordinary use of unaccented syllables, where, at the close of a line, an accented one is required (whether that be the final syllable itself, or with other syllables after it redundant), shows a singular want of comprehension of true rythm and a defect of ear that I can scarcely now account for, although it is not an uncommon occurrence where poets used to rhyme attempt to do without it.   In fine, his version (if it may be estimated by the samples given by his eulogists) is not even respectable, and, from a man of his taste, is, in a bad sense, surprising.   Yet in the passage above quoted, which the newspaper-man, with affected transport, calls " superb ", telling us that *its marvelous words thrill over every nerve of the reader !* (^{a}) there is nothing difficult at all, either of comprehension or of rendering.

Having, in *Arthur Carryl*, given a translation of certain scraps there cited of Dante, and given them, according to my constant custom, in the measure of the original, and with corresponding or equivalent rhymes, years before Mr. L. attempted his version, I hope I have some right to put forward my own rendering of the place, not to show how well it may be done, but to show that it may be done, and easily too, better than he has done it.   These are the lines, written after running over the absurd and pedantic panegyric I have, for my readers' sake as well as for my own, held up to ridicule, and the contempt which befits at all times the hypocrisy of literary dilletanteism.

> There sighs, laments, and howlings of deep woo,
> Resounded through that air without a star,
> Wherefore, at first, my tears could not but flow.
> Tongues of all kinds, and horrible words that jar,
> Phrases of suffering, wrath's discordant sound,
> Shrieks and chok'd cries, and smitten hands, that for
> And near made tumult, to and fro rebound,
> Forever in that air's unchanging gloom,
> Like to the sand which eddying winds whirl round.

I do not aver that this exactitude of imitation could be carried out (even with

(^{a}) There is nothing whatever " marvelous " in either words or verse, although there is much that is admirable in both.   This is the pitiful cant of would-be connoisseurs, who before any work of art, from letters to music, affect a rapture proportioned to its celebrity, and endeavor, by guessing at the value of certain points, or by assuming it without guessing, to acquire the reputation of literary acumen.   As for Mr. L.'s translation, it is obvious to any unbiased reader, and certainly to one who has true knowledge of the subject and of verse in general, that three of the lines are the merest prose, while it is a desecration of the song of the Tuscan to render his accurate rythm by the absolutely unmetrical line which is the middle as well as worst of these three :
" *Languages diverse, horrible dialects.*"

him, through his open window, on his Presidential knees, and took care to advertise it to the public. To shut himself in his closet and pray in secret, according to the precept of Christ, would have been putting his rushlight under a bushel and have deprived the God-devoted of the profit of its lustre. What a sacrifice even of modesty will men not make, when exalted above self by the vapor of an ebullient patriotism!

It was perhaps for his sanctity that this intended martyr, who had had the self-denial to run from destiny in his wife's petticoat, was recently cheered on 'Change in Liverpool. It was certainly not because he recommended his State to dishonor its own bonds, nor because he endorsed for consideration the proposition to murder Lincoln, nor that he claimed to make the cornerstone of his temple of human rights the absolute negation of human liberty, that our cousins of England forgot they had just found out how much they loved us.

6.—P. 414. *No, none of us are so squeamous.*] It is probably, not from habitual vulgarity, but from love of antiquity and his familiarity with old English writers, that the *Cryer's* man uses this, now unjustly considered barbarous and corrupt, form of the word "squeamish." Webster, whom I have so often occasion to find fault with, has absurdly the hypothesis, "Probably from the root of *wamble.*" Chaucer wrote *squaimous;* and his erudite editor tells us: " Robert of Brunne (in his translation of *Manuel des Pechées,* Ms. Bod. 2078. fol. 46.) writes this word, *esquaimous;* which is nearer to its original, *exquamiare,* a corruption of *excambiare.*" TYRWHITT: Gloss. Chauc. *ad v.* In *Rich. Cœr de L.* (ed. Weber,) it is written *squoymous:* "Frendes, be not squoymous, etc.," when the Saracens have the heads of their friends placed in the dishes before them. This is precisely, in its signification, the modern *squeamish.*

single rhyme as here) through the whole of the *Commedia,* but I am positive that without such imitation, though one may give the measure of the poet, he cannot render his *tone,* which is to his stanzas what the coloring is to a fine painting in which that quality is prominent.

7.—P. 420. *You have lost, sir and ma'am, each the nice speciality,*
etc.] Fledgling is, like most imperfectly educated persons who are
literary pretenders, not always to be held responsible for verbal in-
novations; but, in the present instance, he is not so far out of the
way, this form of the substantive — *speciality* for *specialty* — though
not used, being in perfect analogy with that of the words it rhymes
with in the text. Besides, it is correcter etymologically, the term
having come in to us from the French, *spécialité*, used in the same
sense.

P.S. Since the note was written, I have found the word in the
form 'speciality' in a philosophical treatise of the present day; in
Dr. David Page's Essay on "Man," p. 153, N. Y. ed. 1868, — unless
it is there a misprint.

8.—P. 422. *What a phrase is that!*] See above, note 4.

For the allusion to Fernando, there is in a cognate Review of
similar pretensions to those of Dr. Sus's, a passage which will perhaps explain it. As a few years hence men might grope in vain for
its fossilized existence, I shall go to the expense of printing the
article entire, and with all its curiosities of word, syllable and point,
as I find them on pp. 415–417 of the XIVth vol. of *The National
Quarterly Review, Edited by Edward I. Sears, A.M., LL.D.* — The
footnotes are made to supply what the Doctor in his "friendly and
benevolent spirit" constrained himself to suppress.

" *Calvary — Virginina. Tragedies.* By LAUGHTON OSBORN. 12mo., pp. 200.
      New York : Doolady. 1857.

  "In general Mr. Doolady exhibits considerable judgment in his selections; it
is but seldom that we have had any serious fault to find with his publications.
Nor does the one now before us form an exception; although we do not think
that Laughton Osborn will ever occupy a high rank among tragic writers. He
may succeed in other departments of literature, but we can assure him in all
kindness that tragedy is not his forte; nor is poetry in any form. After making
full allowance for the disadvantage under which he has labored in treating the

subjects he has chosen, we see nothing to justify us in the opinion that he would have succeeded under more favorable circumstances.

"The incidents which he has attempted to dramatise in 'Calvary' are at once too familiar and too mysterious. Even Milton has failed in his 'Paradise Regained.' The life and death of Christ are so fully detailed in the New Testament that it would require a genius of a high order to invest the subject with that air of novelty which is essential to the drama. This is admirably illustrated in the *Divina Commedia* of Dante, although not a drama in the strict sense of the term. There is no intelligent person who has read that truly sublime poem who has not observed a vast difference between the *Purgatorio* and the *Paradiso*; but a still greater difference between the *Inferno* and the *Paradiso*, the latter being greatly inferior to either of the former.

"The reason is obvious enough; while neither sacred nor profane history has much to say on what passes in purgatory or hell, each is quite copious on what relates to paradise considered as the happiness derived by man from the death of Christ.

"If however, it be urged that paradise is not familiar, being *extra terram*, the same claim cannot be made for Calvary. That the events which took place at Calvary were in the highest degree tragic is beyond dispute; but, as already observed, all the incidents and circumstances that led to it are so fully described that but little room is left for the exercise of the fancy. Were it otherwise, we think there would still be some objection to the exhibition of Jesus, the Archangels, Mary, the mother of Jesus, Mary Magdalene Simon Peter, &c., on the stage, at least in the style in which it is done in Laughton Osborn's 'Calvary.' *

"Milton was content to commence his Paradise Lost with what took place on our own sphere — 'man's first disobedience,' &c. Homer soared no higher at the outset than the wrath of Achilles. Nor has Virgil attempted a different course. But our present author lays his first scene in heaven, and his first speakers are Raphael and Michael, who have a chorus of angels, though, in sooth, rather a discordant one. In Scene III. Jesus, Mary and Martha appear, the *locus* being 'A room in the dwelling of Jesus' Mother.' If the dialogue which takes place between the Saviour of mankind and his Mother had been intended for a burlesque it could hardly have seemed to us more profane. But we cheerfully do the author the justice to believe that he means well throughout. Mary addresses Jesus, 'O my darling!' and tells him that what He says is to happen

---

* If the reader should think it incredible that the fool, who wrote this stuff, actually supposed that a drama like *Calvary* (even if such was the author's intention) could, with its angels and devils, its scenes in Heaven and in Hell, and the act of the crucifixion, be put upon the stage, in any style, I can only tell him that I copy literally, and I did not make the fellow's brains.

makes her 'blood curdle'.* In another part of the same dialogue she is made
to say:

> 'I am thy mother, Jesus, and my heart
> Warms to thee now as when I first behold thee
> After my weary travail,' &c. — (p. 9.) †

"When Martha enters Mary appeals to her, as if she had more influence on
Jesus than herself, thus:

> 'Kneel with me, Martha! *He has love for thee.*
> Tell him he kills me! Tell him! ——' ‡

"The first scene of the second act is laid in hell, and the interlocutors are
Lucifer and Beelzebub, who have a chorus of evil spirits which differs very
slightly, if anything, from the chorus of angels, except that the former is, perhaps, a little more lugubrious than the latter. Next come Judas Iscariot and
Mary Magdalene. Judas speaks quite idiomatically. 'Ugh!' he says, 'and the

---

* *Mary.* And canst thou speak with calmness, when my heart
　　　　　Is aching for thee? Jesus, O my son!
　　　　　Think on thy mother, and avoid the storm
　　　　　That now is darkening o'er thee, and whose shadow
　　　　　Makes my blood curdle with the chill of death.
　　　　　For my sake, O my darling!

† *Mary.* Stay yet a little. By that happy time
　　　　　Thou hast thyself remember'd, when these breasts
　　　　　That now are wither'd fed thee from my blood,
　　　　　I do adjure thee! Thou hast call'd me Mother
　　　　　With that sweet voice, although again the tone
　　　　　That is so stern and lofty, when thou speak'st
　　　　　Those riddles that I dare not try to solve,
　　　　　Has aw'd and check'd me, — thou hast call'd me Mother.
　　　　　I am thy mother, Jesus, and my heart
　　　　　Warms to thee now as when I first beheld thee
　　　　　After my weary travail; see me now
　　　　　Embrace thy feet, and pray thee as my god,
　　　　　For my sake, for thy own! ——

‡ *Jesus.* Thou hast spoken, Martha, loyally and well.
　　　　　But, in that faith and wisdom, seest thou not
　　　　　That I should need no warning? Even now
　　　　　The heart that shall betray me is convuls'd
　　　　　With its distracting passions, and the hand
　　　　　Is itching for the silver that shall buy
　　　　　My body for the cross. It is decreed.
　　Mary. Mean'st thou this fully? Canst thou still so calmly
　　　　　Speak what to credit is —— My son! my son!
　　　　　Kneel with me, Martha! He has love for thee.
　　　　　Tell him he kills me! Tell him! —— Jesus, son!
　　　　　Have mercy on me! Save thyself — and me!

lamp looks dying.' She replies : 'Be not displeas'd, dear Judas.' (p. 15.) Fur
ther on in the same dialogue she addresses him :

> 'That starv'd look worries me ; and, oh ! the chill
> Of this unwholesome lodging ! ' — (p. 15.) *

"We have not yet got beyond the second act; and the tragedy extends
to five acts, occupying seventy-four pages. Under these circumstances we
think our readers will excuse us if we cannot proceed any farther in this direc-
tion.

"*Virginina* is a better effort than 'Calvary', but we are very much afraid that
it will not succeed as a tragedy. The Romans, male and female, are made to express themselves considerably more like New Yorkers than is in strict accordance
with the truth of history. The following is a pretty favorable specimen :

> *Icil.* — ' I am Icilius, and should the people
> The sole legitimate source of sovereign rule,
> For that they are the many, and their thews
> Strain to heave up, to prop and keep sustain'd
> The edifice whose chambers ye but fill.' — (p. 103.)

"Fernando Wood could hardly have expressed himself more democratically or

---

> * *Judas.* The night is chilly. Hast thou not a coal
> To feed the brazier ? Not one drop of wine ?
> Ugh ! and the lamp looks dying. Where is gone
> The shekel that I gave thee yesternight ?
> *Magd.* Be not displeas'd, dear Judas. I bestow'd it
> But as the Master seem'd to say we ought :
> I cast it in the Treasury.
>   *Judas.* Like that widow
> Whose paltry mites he made of more account
> Than all the rest, because they were her all.
> So thou must give thy all ! Of many fools
> Of Magdala, thou, Mary, art the best.
> Why not have gone at once to the perfumer's,
> Like thy Bethanian namesake, and anoint
> His yellow locks, or even smear his feet,
> As I have seen thee sweep them oftentimes
> With these long delicate hairs (I could defile them !)
> He would have thought still more of it.
>   *Magd.* For shame !
> Thou speakest of our Lord, the Christ, our King.
> *Judas.* I know not that : I know that I am weary
> Of waiting for his kingdom, which I thought
> Would make us rich at least, — both thee and me.
> That starv'd look worries me : and oh, the chill
> Of this unwholesome lodging ! With that shekel
> Thou might'st have bought us fire and light and food.

more patriotically than this when a candidate for Governor of the State.* We cheerfully admit, however, that there are some good passages in Virginia, but we hope we shall be excused if we prefer to let the reader discover them for himself.

"Before we conclude we beg to give the author one word of advice, which we trust he will accept in the same friendly, benevolent spirit in which it is offered. He announces to us on one of the fly-leaves of this volume that the two pieces we have just glanced at 'are the first of a series of *nineteen*, which, with the exception of two, are now completed and ready for the press.' This is followed by the titles of ten tragedies and seven comedies! We have no doubt that Mr. Osborn is as much at home in comedy as he is in tragedy; nay, we think he is more successful in exciting laughter even when he does not mean to do so, than he is in drawing forth tears when most tragically inclined. At the same time, we would advise him to withhold his 'Silver Head' and 'Double Deceit' (comedies) until the peo-

> * *Icil.* I am Icilius, and I hold the people
> The sole legitimate source of sovereign rule,
> For that they are the many, and their thews
> Strain to heave up, to prop and keep sustain'd,
> The edifice whose chambers ye but fill.
> Were Appius not your master as our tyrant,
> My hate to your cruel order were not less,
> And, the decemvirate overthrown, Icilius
> Steps on its carcase, to do battle still
> For freedom and the people's rights. Thou hearest: —
> These are my motives. What are thine?
>   *Lucr.* I am
> Lucretius, and the common folk of Rome
> I have in hatred less than in disdain.
> But is there eye so blear'd that sees not Appius
> Striding to sovereign rule across our necks?
> He cring'd to the people, and they set him o'er them.
> He trod them down. He cringes now to us.
> And Rome beholds the guardians of her state
> Become mere servitors to the usurping Ten,
> Whose plural tyranny even now is merging
> Into the singular rule of this bold man.
> I love my order, and will let no Tarquin
> Level its pillars to rear himself a throne.
> These are my motives.
>   *Icil.* And they please me little;
> As does thy purpled tunic, which they suit.
> But thou dost much; for thou 'rt a man; thy tongue
> Fears not to utter what thy soul dares think.

Thus, the language of Icilius, *which is considerably more like that of a New-Yorker than is strictly accordant with the truth of history,* is addressed to one of the proudest of the patricians, and not, as the truthful reviewer would advise us, to the class of people *Fernando Wood harangues when a candidate for the State Governorship.* The misrepresentation however is not greater than that in every other part of the "notice," beginning with "*Virginia*"; but it is probably less intentional, as being the result of stupidity as well as of envy and malevolence.

ple are much more predisposed to laughter than they are at present, and have more time and money to spare."

And such is the critical record of such a poem as *Virginia!* What will the men of the future think of our standing as a cultivated people, and of the literary judgment and the fair-dealing of our critics, when they are told that this flippant, pedantic, ill-digested and badly-written school-exercise, with its low-bred impertinence, its thinly-vailed and hypocritical malignity, and its brazen-faced falsehood, is the sole notice that has been taken of that tragedy in all the number of our Quarterly Reviews?

9.—P. 423. *Which in all countries, as late I said, etc., etc.*] I fear I have been led into plagiarism ; for these identical phrases occur in a work of prodigiously high standing.

"It is almost superfluous to remark," says the author of a review of *Alfieri's Life and Writings*, in the XIVth vol. *N. Y. Nat. Rev.* p. 216, "that Alfieri was not entitled to the degree of Master to which he thus refers ; but degrees have been conferred in all countries and ages in which there are colleges and universities under similar circumstances ; they are conferred at the present day."

It is true, there is scarcely anything but misrepresentation in the whole article, and its literary judgments are only a little worse than its travesty of Alfieri's Italian; but, for the remark about the manner in which degrees are given, we, looking on the cover of the journal, where we read *A.M.*, write "Approved."

10.—P. 423. *In Heide'berg . . . . . A British noble got LL.D. Conferr'd on his horse.*] I had this story on the Neckar, from an Oxford student on his vacation tour. He gave it as an illustration of the freedom with which the German University dispensed its favors. The nobleman handed-in the name of his Bucephalus, and nothing further was asked.

11.—P. 423. *A letter'd ass* — "*haud absurdum est.*" '*T is* facere *well reïpublicæ.*] By a strange coincidence, there is a motto on one of our Reviews, "Pulchrum est bene facere reipublicæ, etiam *bene dicere* haud absurdum est." Some may think it should read *male-dicere.* As Sus says in the text, the words serve to keep his brain-pan soft; and they may be as efficacious in a title-page.

12.—P. 428. *Because Alger in his* Solitude, *etc.*]

" 'The penalty,' says the author, 'affixed to supremely equipped souls is that they must often be left alone on the cloudy eminence of their greatness, amid the lightnings, the stars, and the canopy, commanding the sovereign prospects indeed, but sighing for the warm breath of the vale, and the friendly embraces of men.' . . To come down from the canopy, we should be very glad to know what all this sighing and gnashing of teeth is about. * * Byron without his mask was a very ordinary sort of person. * * It is indisputable that he liked women ["God help the wicked!"], especially if they were the wives of other men, and the poor heart-broken poet saw a chance to destroy the happiness and blacken the good fame of a quiet household [!]. He pretended to cling to an early attachment, but if he had married the young lady [which?] it is more than probable that he would have treated her as badly, as wickedly, as brutally as he actually treated the lady whose life was cursed by her union with him. The real extent of the baseness of his conduct toward Lady Byron will never be known now, but the one or two who did know of it [know it] declare that it was monstrous beyond conception [!!]. It was no woman's jealousy or pique which darkened poor Lady Byron's days. Those who remember the hints thrown out in a narrative of her life which appeared a few years ago in the London *Daily News* [therefore perfectly reliable] will not need to be informed that the melancholy poet was capable of the vilest acts. He had many less culpable faults [than these "vilest acts" presumed from "hints"]. He liked pleasure [naughty fellow!]. He drank, he gambled, he was consumed with vanity [and drank to cool himself], he had intrigues with men's [not boys'] wives and boasted of them, he turned round and abused his dupes in his poetry for being false to their husbands [eh?], he lied habitually, and he was mean and cunning [all of which propensities, acts, and habits, form what are so curiously called *less culpable faults*]." *N. Y. Times,* Thursday, May 2, 1867.

Alger did indeed talk like a fool, if his style is as above quoted; but this is to grunt and growl like a beast.

13.—P. 428. *And Emerson's verse without rhyming close, And a devilish deal less tough.*]

"The longest poem in the present collection is entitled 'May-Day'. . . . . It *breathes* throughout the freshness and the beauty of Spring, and *overflows* with poetic thought and imaginative *sympathy with the breaking of the* '*marble sleep*' of Winter. [Good lack-a-day! where is Alger?] . . . What a graphic piece of description is this:

> Lo! how all the tribes combine
> To rout the flying foe.
> See, every *patriot* oak-leaf throws
> His elfin length upon the snows;
> Not idle, since the leaf all day
> Draws to the spot the solar ray,
> Ere sunset quarrying inches down,
> And half-way to the mosses brown:
> While the grass beneath the rime
> Has hints of the propitious time,
> And upward pries and perforates
> Through the cold slab a thousand gates,
> Till green lances peering through
> Bend happy in the welkin blue." *N. Y. Times,* May 1, 1867.

The *grass having hints, and prying and perforating in a slab a thousand gates,* and *lances peering* and *bending happy,* is so good that we will cut off this quotation here. Then:

"The northward procession of the Spring is thus vividly described:

> I saw the bud-crowned Spring go forth,
> Stepping daily onward north
> To greet staid ancient *cavaliers*
> Filing single in stately train.
> And who, and who *are* the *travelers!*
> They *were* Night and Day, and Day and Night,
> Pilgrims wight *with step forthright.*
> I saw the Days deformed and *low,*
> *Short* and bent by cold and snow;
> The merry Spring threw wreaths on them,
[Which was a *mauvaise plaisanterie,* as they were already snow-bowed]
> Flower-wreaths gay with bud and bell;
> Many a flower and many a gem,
> *They were refreshed by the smell.*
> They shook the snow from hats and shoon,
> They put their April raiment on;
> *And those eternal forms* ["deformed and low"]

> *Unhurt by a thousand storms*
> [Yet bent by the weight of snow]
> > *Shot up to the height of the sky again,*
> > And danced as merrily as young men."

Fancy them, these *pilgrims wight* with *step forthright,* *shooting up to the height of the sky,* then *dancing away right merrily :* The image is of Longinistic sublimity, and one is tempted to ask with the big-worded Grecian, *Where the devil did they find the space?* But let us continue : it is such a treat to have a pretentious and affected philosopher writing — well, such verses as a child should be spanked for.

> " I saw them mask their awful glance
> *Sidewise meek in gossamer lids ;*
> And to speak my thought if none forbids,
> It was as if *the eternal gods,*
> *Tired of their starry periods,* [acc. *periods'*]
> Hid their majesty in cloth
> *Woven of tulips and painted moth.*
> On carpets green the *maskers* marc't
> Below May's well-appointed arch,
> *Each star, each god, each grace artain,*

[all made out of the *pilgrims wight,* who, vailing *their awful glance's* light, *Sidewise meek,* if no sense *forbids, in gossamer lids,* *maskers* grow in a Joseph's *cloth Woven of tulips and painted moth.* — By the by, as moths do not come out in April, with paint or without, nor the tulips either I believe, where did the *cavalier-traveler-Days deformed* get their wardrobe *Unhurt by a thousand storms* for their *eternal* sky-high *forms ?*]

> Every joy and *virtue speed,* [?]
> Marching duly in her train,
> And *fainting* Nature at her need
> Is made *whole* again."
> [It 's a wonder she was not driven stark-mad.]

And the fool or sycophant praises this stuff of Emerson's, who, besides having his head half-way up in a Swinburne fog, and being almost as incapable of rythm as Walt Whitman, has no adequate conception of what is rhyme !

> " We give space to one extract more, the closing passage of the poem.
> > For thou, O Spring ! canst renovate
> > All that high God did first create.

> Be still his *arm and architect,*
> Rebuild the ruin, mend defect;
> *Chemist* to *vamp* old worlds with new,
> *Coat sea* and sky with heavenlier blue,
> New-tint the plumage of the birds,
> And *slough decay* from grazing herds, etc."

We shall follow no further. The image of the *chemist* turned cobbler and *vamping old worlds with new,* though he does not tell how the feat is done, which were a considerable one even were it *old shoes with new,* and the *sloughing of decay* from cattle while grazing (an excellent thing in the present panic of the meat-market,) make too delectable an ending for us to mar it by addition.

14. —P. 428. *As pompous an ass as Victor Hugo,* Who, etc., etc.] One of the best-marked personal traits of this greatly overrated poet and romancer, is conspicuous in the following note taken from the *N. Y. Times* of July 30, 1867.

"Letter from Victor Hugo on John Brown.
From la Coöpération.
The editor of this journal, having opened a subscription with a view to offering a medal to JOHN BROWN's widow, received the subjoined letter from VICTOR HUGO:

Hauteville House, July 3, 1867.
Sir: My name belongs to all who would make use of it to serve progress and truth.
A medal to LINCOLN calls for a medal to JOHN BROWN. Let us cancel that debt pending such time as AMERICA shall cancel hers. America owes JOHN BROWN a statue as tall as that of WASHINGTON. WASHINGTON 'founded' America, JOHN BROWN diffused liberty.
I press your hand.

VICTOR HUGO."

Here we see lack of judgment in the exaltation of a simple fanatic, relieved, but not concealed, by a pomposity and affectation that are really ludicrous. Much of what M. Hugo writes in epistles to the public is of this character: (witness his appeal for Maxi-

milian to Juarez.*)   He seems to think himself not only the primi-
tive and particular apostle of liberty, but the foremost man on all
occasions, and whose sentiments on any public question are of
value, whether he is conversant with it or not.   Yet it is this affectation, which would degrade even ordinary talent, and reminds us
of the stage-strut and mouthing of secondrate tragedy-actors, that
is taken, by such asses as *Fledgling*, (though in the text he is not
made to bray) as a proper indication of genius.   For example:

"The recent correspondence between Victor Hugo and the young poets of
France . . . . is one of the most graceful and eloquent passages in modern literature. * * * To their expressions of ' boundless admiration' the old poet replied
with a delicacy of compliment, a brilliancy of eloquence, a tenderness of feeling
which showed how well they had called him 'master', and how simply and [yet]
boldly true were their epithets. 'Dear poets, the literary revolution of 1830,
corollary and consequence of the revolution of 1789 [!], is a fact which belongs to
our age. I am the humble soldier of this progress. I fight for revolution under
all its forms — under the literary form as under the social form. I have liberty for
principle, progress for law, the ideal for type.' Our epoch is 'a profound epoch,
against which no reaction is possible. Grand art forms a part in this grand age.
It is its soul. * * We, the old — we have had the combat ; you, the young —
you will have the triumph.' Then, in a characteristic generalization, Victor Hugo
declares that ' the *spirit of the 19th century* combines the *democratic search for* the
True, with the *eternal law* of the Beautiful', and it directs 'everything toward
this sovereign end, liberty in intelligence, the ideal in art. Literature ought to
be *at once democratic and ideal : democratic for civilization, ideal for the soul*.'"
(*N. Y. Times.*)

   All of which is as pellucid as plumcake, while at the same time it
is as void of inflation as soap-bubbles.

"In a fine closing sentence," pursues the newspaper youth, "he tells the young
poets, 'I am proud to see my name surrounded by yours. Your names are a
garland of stars'" [of the smallest microscopic magnitude.]

---

* And more recently his vehement objurgation of those who chose to sentence
and to execute a negro girl of twelve years, who had committed a murder in
Kentucky.   The newspapers make him eject froth after this fashion : "Was
there not manhood left in Kentucky to tear out the tongues of the fiends who
pronounced judgment on that girl, and break the arms of those who were base
enough to carry out such a sentence ?"   Yet M. Hugo has long ceased to be a
schoolboy.

Perhaps he wrote *galaxy*. But it does not matter. Either way, simple or confused, the metaphor is felicitous. If they are the stars, he of course must be the centre of the system; and that he could assert them to be such, and proclaim his own pride to be so garlanded, galaxied, or satellited, is especially illustrative of the "*democratic search for the True*," — which no one will henceforth doubt has been found by M. Hugo.

15.—P. 435. ACT THE THIRD.] In this Scene, if I shall seem to praise myself, it will be because I copy, as closely as the occasion and the verse will permit, the sentiments expressed by two of the characters in their literary function, and the facts as detailed to one of my brothers by the third.

In taking the liberty I have done in introducing these gentlemen into my piece, I have been guided more by a sense of gratitude than by any other motive. I have so little to be grateful for in all my literary career to my fellows, that I may be allowed to indulge the feeling at the expense of an appearance of egotism, as I certainly have done it to the detriment of my drama.

Begging then pardon of each one, I may say to him safely, if I know myself:

> "In freta dum fluvii current, ...
> . . . . polus dum sidera pascet,
> Semper honos, nomenque tuum, laudesque manebunt,
> Quae me cumque vocant terrae."

16.—P. 439. *Because intent   To keep from the light his false argument.*]

> Who shames a scribbler? break one cobweb through,
> He spins the slight, self-pleasing thread anew:
> Destroy his fib, or sophistry, in vain,
> The creature's at his dirty work again. POPE. *Prol. to Sat.*

Just as this 3d Act was passing through the hands of the com-

positor, I learned that the *Round Table* had, with inconceivable
effrontery — no, it was the *Round Table* — had, with characteristic
effrontery, dared to talk thus of *Bianca* — of *Bianca Capello*, which
I have placed next to *Virginia* in the collective volume of dramas, —
Bianca, which, however faulty, is full of incident, action and passion,
and conspicuous for stage-effect, but whose "plot" is its weakest
point, and whose "language and ideas" this sciolist, who cannot
write grammatically and has no sentiment but for the commonplace
and routine of his trade, condemns by commendation. The empha-
sizing by capitals and italics is my own.

"There is the *same tiresome prolixity of dialogue*, the *same* PECULIAR WOOD-
ENNESS IN THE PERSONAGES of the drama, the *same* FRIGIDITY OF IMAGINA-
TION we before remarked as *characteristic of the author*, but also, it is fair to
add [delightful candor!], a symmetry of plot and, *in the main*, a correctness of
language and ideas which are his chief virtues. The play is founded on an *episode in the* romantic *history* of Bianca Capello, who, etc." [It happens to be her
entire history. Did he really know what is an "episode?"] "She died in 1587,
at *Poggio* [Did she? It would be as correct to say, The ducal palace was *at
Pitti*. She died in the Villa del Poggio *at Caiano*, as he was taught in the drama,
as well as in the "Appendices" from which alone the dunce has borrowed all his
information] within *a few minutes* of her husband, [that is the play, not history,
which the ignorant is affecting to talk after. The briefest interval assigned by
historians is *fifteen hours*] both having been taken suddenly ill after a dinner *at*
which the grand duke's brother, Cardinal Ferdinand, *participated*." [*Participated at* is good. Here is a smatterer, who pretends to find correctness (I beg
pardon, *correctness in the main*) in my language, yet cannot write an article,
occupying in its whole extent about half a column of his miscellany, without making three capital mistakes in his own; for when he says, in the title of the book,
"Being *a* completion of the First volume, &c.", he wrote what I did not. Had I
so chosen to phrase the title, I should have said "*the* completion;" but it is
really printed "Being *in* completion."] "The cardinal was suspected of having
poisoned them, a view which Mr. Osborn adopts, making the motive consist *in
his unrequited love for Bianca*." Etc., etc. [Mr. Osborn never made any such
thing. He is not a fool, though his cacocritic may be half-a-dozen. But this
assertion must be deliberate, therefore wilful, misrepresentation, — like that of
the *Nation* when it said I made Judas sell his Master to buy Mary Magdalene

bread and butter. The Cardinal, blinded by revenge for a supposed injury, the most poignant that could be offered to a man of his temper as well as of his position, permits Malocuor, the inventor of that simulated wrong, to poison both the Duke and Bianca in order to further his the Cardinal's long-brooded ambition. A reader of nature, — which is not either the *Round Table's* waiter or the old woman of the *Nation*, — knows well that it is often these added stings that give the final impulsion to some vicious passion, and prompt to a sudden and violent accomplishment what has been the meditated purpose of years.]

Let us return to the criticism (so to call it). " Prolixity of dialogue " is hardly reconcileable with "symmetry of plot " and " correctness of language and ideas." The dramatist who exhibits these striking merits could not easily commit a fault which can exist only with one who is ignorant of the requirements of dramatic writing. *Symmetry of plot*, if I understand the phrase, implies strict unity of action, and therefore the exclusion of everything that would impede, or even be unnecessary to, that action. Upon this principle, I may be suffered to assert, are all my dramas founded,* and therefore I shall be found to set aside all the useless, awkward, and unnatural train of confidants, and persons whose whole business in a play is to talk, whether wit or wisdom, and whose intervention does not promote one step the evolution of the plot or the approach

---

* I must be forgiven, if, with considerable hesitation, I venture to append from *Ernestin* (published 1858), the following passage, which I am willing should furnish the standard whereby my dramas are to be measured, although in fact it had reference only to *Virginia*.

. . . . "for the same spirit of truth which guided Ernestin in all things else made him shrink, as at sin, from any violation of probability in the plot, shaped his characters with consistency and exactness, and rendered impossible a want of nature in the dialogue ; while the energy, impetuosity, and fire of his disposition, which in everything he undertook was ever driving him to the end by the straightest and shortest road and without abatement of speed, saved him from irrelevance of incident and superfluousness of persons, shut out all narrative that was not unavoidable, and made his action and his style rapid, vehement, and nervous." p. 348.

This, it may be thought, is high self-praise. But, looking down the not dim vista of the future, and seeing what I there see in its far horizon, the single star that never sets on my grave, I do not fear to write it, and boldly challenge for it the exactest scrutiny.

of the catastrophe. And it is on this account I have said above, that the 3d Act, though introduced with a particular design, spoils the present piece. Having too, I well may claim, an absolute devotion to Nature, sacrificing all needless description, all poetical adornment, where contrary to her requirements, how is it possible that my dialogue should be prolix? Besides, the *Table* knows very well, or there is another point deficient in its qualifications, that in every play extensive mutilations are made in the dialogue to fit it for the Stage.* But the reader shall judge for himself. Bound up in this volume, is the *Montanini*, a drama fitted for performance. If I shall be found to have uttered there any five lines in succession that could have been spared, I will admit the Table-man is less reckless of his assertions in one particular than he appears to be in all.†

For the "peculiar woodenness in the personages": where the

---

* *Vide passim* Inchbald's British Theatre.—I have indicated, myself, some of the abbreviations to be made in my own dramas.

† In the favorite tragedy of *Hamlet*, which has twenty-two interlocutors, great and small, I make out 3482 verses, of all kinds, counting among them the lines of prose dialogue, each of which contains rather more word-matter than a full iambic verse. In *Virginia*, which has twenty interlocutors, whereof sixteen have perfectly distinctive characters, there are 1690 verses, 31 of which are marked "to be omitted" in the representation. Deducting these, there are but 1659 verses. Thus Shakspeare's *Hamlet* has 1823 verses, or actually one-half, more of dialogue than *Virginia!* Nay, *Bianca Capello*, which covers a period of many years (being a "romantic" drama) and has thirty-three speakers, great and small, contains but 2524 verses all told, or, deducting those marked *to be omitted* (98 in number,) 2426 verses, being 1056 (or nearly one-third) less than in *Hamlet*.

So much for the integrity of this —— Poh! where the deliberate misrepresentation, the crafty mutilation and suppression, the hypocritical depreciation, are so prominent characteristics of all the *Round Table's* notices, beginning with that of *Virginia*, it is but a small matter to find it thus demonstrably false-spoken. The reader will however understand that were my books not kept from circulation, nay *virtually suppressed*, by the malignant calumnies of such mean pretenders, I should not extend to them the honor of an argument, and the *School for Critics* would not take the place of pieces which, like the *Montanini*, do something more than furnish amusement.

proud, yet hypocritical and subtle *Cardinal*, the crafty, double-dealing and perfidious *Malocuore*, the grave, dignified, sensible and honorable *Sennuccio*, the impulsive yet gallant *Bonaventuri*, and Bianca herself, tender, yet spirited and high-minded, are prominent,— where even the very *Assassins* have each his distinctive character, and there is no one without attribute save *Donna Virginia*, who is purposely made so, and is so indicated in the text, — where these and others are the persons represented, the man who could dare say that must be either ignorant of his trade — I beg pardon, he is perfectly master of his trade — ignorant, then, of true criticism, or a wilful falsifier. Let him be either or both. Probably as both he is useful in a journal which, according to its own modest and truthful account of itself in its "*spontaneous* growth," "has labored vigorously for national literature" and has been "pronounced to be the Ablest Publication of its Class in the United States."* I venture the assertion, without any hesitancy (because I speak after due comparison), that, whatever the defects of my pieces, there are not, in the whole range of dramatic writing from Æschylus down, any series of *characters* that are better discriminated, more life-like, and more true to nature than my own.

For the "frigidity of imagination", I have said enough in the 3d Act of this drama, — p. 436, lines 4–7, and p. 438, il. 12–18. The fool or malignant who ventured on that false ascription would, were his censure conscientious, exclude Schiller, Alfieri, Corneille from the Pantheon of dramatic poets and put Bedlam Swinburne in its principal niche. It is the old story. Pope, who, aiming at "correctness," had sense for his lodestar and reason for his monitor, is

---

* One thing is certain. Either the writer of that article is a born fool, or he is a parcel-educated dullard. I had a brief acquaintance with the late Edgar A. Poe. On one occasion, when I was speaking of the unpopularity of my works, he said to me: "We authors, Mr. Osborn, have opinions of our own, and they are in general very different from those that are retailed to the public by reviewers." Such is my consolation.

denied by such men the spirit of a poet: the genuine bards are those
alone who give rein to their hippogriff and gallop up and down the
poetical heaven just as the ungovernable mongrel may choose to bear
them. The first principle of good writing is perspicuity. He whose
"imagination" sees clearly will paint clearly, and his words, like
the colors and the tones of a true painter, will not be of the rainbow,
nor of the cloud, but pure, distinct, harmonious; his light and shadow,
though magical in their attraction, will be nature's own, and his design, while free of harshness, in no part vague. The lessons of criticism seem to be excluded from our schools, or to be forgotten. Yet
the principles of true art are the same as they were a hundred years
ago, and will be the same forever, for they are founded on nature
and reason only. Who are the poets that are still preferred? For
one who reads, or better, who has redd Lycophron, there are ten
thousand who joy in Homer still. How is it then, that that which
is so much admired in the latter, his simplicity and distinctness,
should allow of admiration for the glittering fustian of a Talfourd or
the unintelligible jumble of a Swinburne? But such writers are not
really admired, and are never understood. It argues perspicacity,
to pretend to understand them. *Omne ignotum pro mirifico:* what is
not intelligible is taken to be wonderful. In the words of my own
text (let me be permitted to repeat them:)

> For fustian maintains *a name's* illusion
> With man, who is dazzled by word-confusion,
> And finds magnificent and grand
> All that his noddle can't understand,
> And weighty the thoughts from whose tangled skeins
> He fails to draw a conclusion.

Frigidity of imagination, or of anything else, in *me!* —— But the
impertinent did not believe, and never even thought it. It was a
tumid phrase of abusive hemi-criticism, and he used its sound, as
fustianists and magpies do, without a meaning. But, when I say,
that to have used it shows he has frigidity of heart and arctic iciness

of conscience, I speak thoughtfully, and mean (with allowance for the stilted language I mimic but to mock) precisely what I say.*

That the reader might know what these creatures are, and that the future may have no trouble to unearth them, I have taken these pains to notice what would otherwise be speedily forgotten. The day will come when the malignant, envious and perhaps revengeful author of that short-sighted article will hide his head for having ejected it on such a tragedy as *Bianca*, as the gentlemen I have ventured to introduce in the present piece as the interlocutors of Act III. will take honor to themselves that they had the sense to feel, the taste and culture to understand, and the conscience to express their judgment and their feeling, in the case of all these dramas, which not ten thousand fools and maliguants can put down, and which shall take their place in my country's literature in defiance of the neglect of her men of real talent and the studied slight of her fifteen-penny criticasters. Living but for truth, as perhaps I shall die for it, one great desire of my life is to represent as they are these parasites on the fair growth of literature, to show them in their actual deformity, their individual insignificance and yet their aggregate noxiousness. — Let me annex but one remark:

If anything could increase my disgust, or add to the turpitude of the pretentious sheet thus noticed, it is that in the leading article of this very Number, it lends its influence to promote the election, to the Presidency of this great republic, of a man who was a traitor to its unity, and not only the abettor of treason, but who had the baseness to address in friendly terms the horrible wretches whose hands were scarcely dry of the innocent blood with which they had sprinkled the ashes of incendiarism and dyed of a more revolting hue the crime

---

* I beg leave to refer to a subnote "(4)" in the 3d Appendix to *Bianca*. The melancholy avowal there made would have moved any but the "frigid" nature I expose to scorn. Yet the heartless blockhead culled out of it an allusion (*After my death, when my countrymen may condescend to read these dramas,*) wherewith to make a gnat's sting of the last of his Lilliputian arrows.

22*

of burglary.   But why should I be disgusted?   It was meet that the false-tongued journal, which in envy, malice, or in downright ignorance, could lend itself to the overthrow of the temple of true art, should look with complacency on treason, and find no danger to the republic in the advocates or apologists of rebellion and the demagogism that would truckle to the worst passions of a foreign-born mob.

17.—P. 440.   *For he took the pains both pieces to cite   In a note to his story of* Alice.]   *Hinc illae lacrymae.*   Had I kissed the rod, I might have counted more sugarplums both for Alice and for Bianca. But the temptation to expose the ignorance, the self-assurance, the flippant impertinence, the hypocrisy, the mendacity, of these animated fungi of literature, was too mighty to resist.   So I succumbed, without a permit from Doolady.

18.— P. 442.   *Val Jean in the Misérables, — Who, liken'd to Christ in the strife for good* —]   This is not my comparison.   The more reverent reader will please hold M. Hugo responsible.

19.—P. 447.   *Like 'Ferdinand Mendez Pinto Dixon   Who found,* etc.]   Malice is contagious.   Inoculated with the virus of Mr. Hepworth Dixon's slanders, the *Vie Parisienne,* which the correspondent of the *N. Y. Times* (whence I take the translation) says is an able weekly paper circulating among the better classes of Paris, has the audacity to talk as follows :

"In conclusion, I hardly dare to speak of a certain trait of American manners, it is so delicate ; but I am going to risk it.   It appears that there is *a* house at New York, tolerated by the *Government* [!], where they satisfy the wishes of married ladies who do not care for the joys of maternity.   A lady, in making her morning calls, tells her friends that on a certain day she had been to the house in question, with as much indifference as if it had been a work of charity.   Young ladies are also taken into this house to board, who — but I stop, and for a good cause.   When one reflects that an act which carries the people who commit it *so far away from France* [!] appears quite natural in America, he cannot but have a strange opinion of *universal* morality."   *July* 30, 1867.

But for the atrocious advertisements which abound in the New-
York newspapers, in none more than in the *N. Y. Times* itself, it is
easy to see that such a wicked absurdity, wherein combine the ignorance, the malice, and the self-conceit, that distinguish in literary
matters the " ingenious gentlemen " of the *Round Table*, could never
have been concocted.   But if not purely the invention of the writers
in either case, they have been the victim's of a well-known danger-
ous humor among our people, — that of bantering supercilious
strangers, and stuffing their ears with all sorts of libels against
themselves.   This has been recognized by all of us as practiced on
all the note-taking travelers, beginning with Mrs. Trollope and including the cockney Dickens.

I may add, that the most impertinent of the transgressions of
these Munchausens is their pretence of describing the most refined
society among us as if they were familiar with it, whereas I have
never been able to discover that they were in it at all; not at least
in New York.

20.—P. 449.   *Save one divine article   Of which not a particle
Shall be lost to the last of the Yankees begotten.*]   See above, Note 8,
where it will be found preserved, like the fly in amber.

21.—P. 453.   — skedaddled —]   See next note.

22.—P. 459.   — vamos'd the ranch !]   A mongrel cant phrase
prevalent in the South-west.   *Vamos* is the Spanish for *Allons !
Come !* and *ranche* is a corruption of *rancho*, or *rancheria*, which in
the Mexican-Spanish of California appears to be used to signify a
farm, although in the Castilian application of the word (*mess*, or
mess-room) the composition is intelligible.   The phrase is therefore
equivalent to the kindred elegancies, *absquatulated* — " skedaddled "
— and the English, as well as American, "cut stick."   All of which
niceties we gather from the newspapers, if they teach us nothing

else ; and for which, as they are characteristic of our hero S. M., and his congeners, let us be thankful.

23.—P. 462.   *But dotes on Walt Whitman's batrachian fire —*]

" Walt Whitman's 'Carol of Harvest, for 1867,' is a very unequal production. The opening stanzas are *overflowing with poetic feeling,* and their *rythm is sweet and musical. How tender is the pathos of these lines :*

*   *   *   *

Pass—pass, ye proud brigades !
So handsome, dress'd in blue—with your tramping, sinewy legs ;

*   *   *   *

Pass ; — then rattle, drums, again !
Scream, you steamers on the river, out of whistles loud and shrill, your salutes !
For an army heaves in sight—O another gathering army !
Swarming, trailing on the rear—O you dread accruing army !
O you regiments so piteous, with your mortal diarrhœa ! with your fevers !
O my land's maimed darlings ! with the plenteous bloody bandage and the crutch !
Lo ! your pallid army follow'd !

But on these days of brightness,
On the far-stretching beauteous landscape, the roads and lanes, the high-piled
    farm-wagons, and the fruits and barns,
Shall the dead intrude ?

*   *   *   *   `   *

Melt, melt away, ye armies ! disperse, ye blue-clad soldiers !
Resolve ye back again—give up, for good, your deadly arms ;
Other the arms, the fields henceforth for you, or South or North, or East or West,
With saner war — sweet wars — life-giving wars.

" But the following passage " (says the criticaster tenderly) . . . " *reads more like* an extract from an agricultural report than poetry :

*   *   *

The engines, thrashers of grain, and cleaners of grain, well separating the straw,
The power-hoes for corn fields — the nimble work of the patent pitchfork ;
Beholdest the newer saw-mill, the cotton-gin, and the rice-cleanser."
— *N. Y. Times,* Aug. 20, 1867.

After that, the honest and capable criticizer notices some of Mr. Tilton's always rythmical verses, and says, "Such verses might be written *by the yard,* and *kept on hand to be cut into pieces* of right [the right] length to fill out a page." Where it will be seen that the ignoramus has uttered what, barring its bad English, might be reasonably applied to Mr. Whitman's *measures.*

24.--P. 466. -- *at Willis'.*] Almack's.

25.--P. 482. *He may rank with New England's best.*] Some persons may think this is not paying him a very great compliment. However that may be, it is a just one. But to pick out the child's trifle, and pass over all the well melodized and often nervous poems that precede it, was quite after the fashion of newspaper and magazine witlings, where they have a personal animosity, and is notably *Fledgling.*

26.--P. 485. " *Hanging to dry.*"] Of so brief a quotation, it is not always easy to trace the source, and consequently to explain the allusion. We are able to do this in the present case, only by going to the familiar associations of the *Hotchpot Cryer.* Deadhead had probably in the cleanly chambers of his memory one of those exhilarating volumes — *Fescennini versus,* which are kept under the tables of the market peddlers and sold with great mystery to schoolboys and servant-maids.

END OF THE FOURTH VOLUME.

www.ingramcontent.com/pod-product-compliance
Lightning Source LLC
Chambersburg PA
CBHW022139020726
47496CB00008B/2464